The Bexford North/Annie Watson Mystery series comprise six books, each complete in itself:

THE BELL TOLLED TWICE

MURDER OF THE INNOCENT. SYDNEY SUMMER: 1943

TONY BRENNAN

Copyright © 2016 Tony Brennan

ISBN: 978-1-925681-19-2

Published by Vivid Publishing
P.O. Box 948, Fremantle
Western Australia 6959
www.vividpublishing.com.au

Cataloguing-in-Publication data is available from the National Library of Australia

Cover photo (bell tower) by Tien Rofe, used with gracious permission.

ACKNOWLEDGEMENTS

My deep and genuine gratitude to Dr PSB for her proof reading and her excellent suggestions. She so often turned my clumsy sentences into something readable

DEDICATION

This one for Duncan

&

The unheralded, often disparaged, unpaid, never-ending work of those groups of women who cared for the unwanted in society – for those whom society had abandoned.
In the 1940s many dedicated groups were active in this valiant work

This is one such story, based on fact.

FOREWORD

I became aware, during my research into the period of the WW2 years in Australia, at the number of illegitimate babies that were being abandoned at Church doors – usually the result of 'one-night-stands' between very young women and soldiers on leave, or just about to go abroad, to war.

The actual number is staggering. I then had to find out who cared for all these abandoned waifs. This led me to study orphanages; especially Church groups which took in these children.

The Christian Churches were very strong during those years; many were engaged in this desperately needed work. However, the Anglican and Catholic Churches cared for the greater number of orphanages. The Catholic ones, for girls, were staffed by different Congregations of Nuns – the Sisters of Mercy and the Sisters of St Joseph seem to have had the largest number. Of the two major Christian denominations, the Catholic ones were the easier, for me, to research, so I concentrated on those. They kept splendid records.

Some of these orphanages were huge affairs; others quite small. Some, obviously, were splendid while others, depending on the personnel, not nearly so fine.

However, on the whole, the nuns – who carried the greater part of the burden – tried desperately to cope, as well as they could, with the enormous numbers of children whom nobody wanted; who were the outcasts of society – through no fault, whatsoever, of their own.

To add to the burden, England dumped ship-loads of illegitimate children on Australia as well – ostensibly to protect them from the war, in reality, just to get rid of them.

Having heard a true story from a very old nun – I think she was over ninety – of one of their 'charges': an innocent, naïve, girl's unwitting involvement with gangsters and the fearful, explosive tragedy that was a result of this - for the Convent. I wanted to use this story to highlight the work of these valiant women.

It is easy to forget, these abandoned children were yet another by-product of that horrendous period of WW2; a problem that had to be faced by those on the home front.

– Tony Brennan

PROLOGUE

The bell engulfed her.

She panted, gasping.

Must run … *No!* ... She *must take* Luke…

The darkness …safer …*That bell*! …

Stop! Why *WON'T* IT STOP?

Little time… she *must* hurry …*Luke! Luke!* …

No! Not *NOW*, Luke! …

NO! …Don't… *please*…Oh dear God! …

She shrieked aloud! …

The bell exploded in an eruption of sound splintering the huge
space into a thousand tiny pieces.

She began to fall slowly

In silence…

… Such… *pain!* …

… *So much blood …so MUCH BLOOD!*

***

The convent waking-bell tolled from the tower over the Chapel.
The nun awoke, her body dripping in sweat; her face twisted in
fear!

1

Frankie, 'Lucky', Falconi was in a foul mood. He trudged through the last section of his weekly collection round, hating it and hating everybody. He felt a strong desire to hurt someone; it didn't matter who it was – anyone would do.

In the late summer of 1944 his area of the city seemed full of American soldiers and sailors, enjoying their R and R. in Sydney. He hated them; but couldn't avoid them: they congregated in large numbers in Lucky's area – Sydney's hot-spot, Kings Cross: the city's red-light district.

Lucky's lips curled in contempt as he listened to the exaggerated, nasal speech of the Americans; it made the native Australian nasal accent appear conservative by contrast.

He shrugged and spat. They were good for trade so he was forced to tolerate them – they filled the brothels his grandfather owned – but, on a personal level, he loathed them; everything about them; their finely pressed, smart, uniforms, their excellent teeth, their boundless self-confidence. They made him feel shabby by comparison and … no one – no one at all – did *that*!

He flushed; painfully aware his clothes, though expensive, were not smart, or well cut – no amount of money could procure what wasn't available.

Yanks! Bloody, Bloody, Yanks! *They* were now the heroes, come to save Australia! *The arrogant bastards!*

Just then, he was jostled by an American sailor – in immaculate whites – looking at him with the contempt reserved for those in civilian clothes.

Lucky's first impulse was to grab the sailor by his shirt front and smash his teeth in; he had done that to others, many times. This time, however, he was hampered by the heavy briefcase he was carrying, so he simply *looked* at the tall, young American.

The sailor, staring into those dangerous, baleful eyes, had apologized quickly and moved on, casting nervous glances over his shoulder as he hurried to get away.

After this encounter, Lucky's spirits rose; he felt better. He was suddenly aware his stomach was growling; he was hungry. His thoughts drifted to a sandwich, or perhaps a pie, maybe two. He made a decision. He'd grab something to eat and take some time out; he would sit in the park near the intersection.

He needed time to think quietly of the suggestion his grandfather, the Falcon, had made before he left the house that morning. Lucky was no fool; Nonno had made it a *suggestion*, but Lucky knew full well that meant it was … an *order*.

He didn't see *how* he could fulfil the request, yet it *had* to be done, one way or another – it didn't do to cross the Falcon, even if he did happen to be his own grandfather.

There was no sentiment involved, dealing with Nonno – he'd sacrifice anyone, in a flash, if it suited his purposes – especially, if he had been disobeyed.

Lucky shut his eyes briefly as he thought of the unleashed fury if he failed.

Lucky thoughts drifted to his mother – that quivering, religious fanatic. He remembered, with a slight shudder, she had only become like that after her husband, Lucky's Babbo – his papa – was put on the 'hit list' by his own father, the Falcon.

And, Lucky thought bleakly, there was the added mystery of his sister, Anna. She had simply vanished – as if she had never existed – and was never ever spoken of again; even by his mother.

She must be dead. He missed her; at one time he had been very fond of her.

A new possibility occurred to him: was it possible she could *still* be alive? How could she just disappear? Someone …somewhere, *must* know.

It wasn't safe to ask … or *was* it? He wondered, if... No …No, too dangerous… leave it. Yes, he decided, she's most probably dead, too, just like Babbo.

Holding the heavy briefcase tightly, Lucky went into a takeaway sandwich shop and walked to the head of the queue. Girls from the local offices and shops, made up the majority of people waiting.

They grumbled, muttering, at someone jumping the queue, but the proprietor, seeing who the customer was, quickly fulfilled his order smilingly and didn't ask for payment when it was completed.

Lucky favoured him with a nod of approval – good lad! He'd remembered.

Lucky noticed the man still had plaster on his cheeks. He'd been right in thinking the bloke would remember better, if he had some scars to remind him – the knife was useful. He smiled, amused, at the thought.

Waiting at the traffic-lights to cross the road to the small park on the opposite side, his eyes suddenly lit up; he smiled briefly and triumphantly.

He wasn't called Lucky for nothing!

He looked carefully across at the young woman – a pretty girl really.

She was sitting alone quietly eating her sandwiches, her knees modestly together, her clothes plain, neat and definitely unfashionable – marking her as *exactly* the type he was looking for, while the obliging late summer sun caught the little gold cross, making it sparkle, at her neck. Lucky felt like shouting aloud.

HE HAD FOUND ONE!

Lucky grinned. This was going to be a pushover! He'd have no need to worry about the Falcon's wrath today. All the protection money had been dutifully collected without too much fuss and here was a bonus all waiting for the knight in shining armour to take home to Nonno!

But, this would need a change of personality – a different approach.

Lucky began to change his personality. His frown smoothed out, his shoulders drooped into an apologetic form and his walk became no longer arrogant; he tilted his head forward slightly, looking at his feet as he walked.

Very soon, the, apparently, diffident, nervous, young man, walked hesitatingly across the main road, carrying his little packet of sandwiches in his hand, after waiting dutifully until the light was correctly green – just like any other good, law-abiding citizen.

He suddenly felt very happy and secure while he stifled his desire to laugh out aloud. The sour mood was gone; he'd always loved acting.

Now he was ready!

2

"Annie, Annie Watson!" Monica Jeffrey called as she caught sight of her cousin being helped down from the back of an army trunk. "What in the name of heaven ...."

'Don't worry, Monica," the older woman shouted. "I've joined the Army; rank of Major, only temporarily, though."

Two of the soldiers, laughing, jumped down and put two large suitcases on the pavement. They then vaulted back into the truck and it took off with a roar, the men laughing and shouting: "Good bye, Mum!"

"Cheeky boys!" replied Annie, waving.

Annie then left the suitcases on the pavement and ran to hug Monica.

"But, the army truck?" Monica was bewildered.

"Thank God for it! These cases weigh a ton."

"But, the Army is not allowed to give civilians a lift, Annie. How did you manage it?"

"Simple, if you know the right people." She noticed the incomprehension on her young cousin's face. "Look, dear child, it's simple; I'll tell you later. Those nice young boys– off to Victoria Barracks – gave me a lift."

"Do you think, Annie, we should move inside; with all the noise, the neighbours are starting to come into their front gardens."

"You'll just have to explain that your cousin has just been

released; tell them she'll settle down once she had her medication – that'll set the tongues wagging."

"I bet. Come on, let's get these damn cases inside and then you can hum and hah and say beautiful things about my wonderful, glorious, exciting and dreamy, new home!"

"That's what the problem is – the house. Monica, you said the house you inherited was in Vaucluse; it's not, it's in Double Bay – the street was right, the suburbs were miles apart."

"Oh, I meant to inform you; I thought I did. After Cousin Ernest's clever work in getting us this house from Mum's will, he definitely said, 'Vaucluse'. It wasn't until we came to see it, that we discovered it's in another suburb altogether. But," she added happily, "we love it. It's even lovelier that the other suburb – at least we think so."

"Now, you tell me! We had a terrible time trying to find it."

The two women picked up the cases and took them inside the beautiful garden. Annie stopped to look at the house.

"Monica, this house is really something. I've been dreading it would be just horribly 'wealthy-looking' and no taste, but it isn't. It's truly beautiful …it's…it's… *grand*! Yes, that's the word: *grand*!" She kissed her cousin. "Thanks be to God, for it, Monica. You've now a wonderful house with plenty of ground for all your kids.

"And, talking of kids. Where are they? You haven't, have you?"

"Haven't?"

"Haven't sold them; have you?'

"Annie!"

"Well, I often wanted to sell my lot, bargain prices, too; no one would take them on."

Monica laughed. "No, three are playing in the garden and the baby is sleeping. Don't wake him for the love of Mike; he has a voice that augurs badly for the future – it sounds like a politician."

The two women moved into the house which, Annie noticed, was richly furnished, then leaving the cases in the hall, went on into the kitchen.

***

Monica Jeffrey was genuinely delighted at the prospect of having these few days with Annie as her guest; she had been so anxious to show her their wonderful new home. The two women were friends, as well as cousins, and since the death of Monica's mother, the Lady Emily Gascoigne-Ridley, their friendship had become stronger than ever.

Sitting at the kitchen table, her hat removed. Annie relaxed and looked at her cousin. "You look wonderful, Monica," Annie cried, "You know, dear girl, you've got the 'family look' – the 'black Irish look' I call it – you, Mother Benedicta and I, have the same large startlingly, deep blue, clear eyes and long lashes, black hair and high cheek bones.

"You and I are frightening alike, except that your hair does what you tell it; mine is always in a state of utter rebellion."

"Well, we've always looked alike, Annie; you look pretty good yourself for…"

"For a woman whose hair is now not only uncontrollable, but going grey."

"No, I wasn't going to say that. You lead too exciting a life to ever grow old."

"So you say; you should see me in the morning; but you …you are positively blooming after the birth of your child." Annie smiled and, this time, spoke softly.

"Truly, Monica it makes me so happy to see you so well – after, well …everything. You have a good husband, four babies now and a wonderful, wonderful new house. On top of that, you look glowing – younger than ever! I'm ever so jealous!"

"Thanks be to God, Annie," responded Monica. "We're so happy in this huge house – we've got room to move." Monica put down her cup of tea.

"Before we go sightseeing, Annie, may I ask what the dickens do you have in those suitcases; they weigh a ton?

"Pumpkins and potatoes, a big book and a life jacket" was the prompt response. "The vegetables are for you; I've so many pumpkins that Sam has threatened divorce if I serve him another helping, while the neighbours are in the same boat. The seasons has been so good this year – we've got pumpkins everywhere.

"We've all been living on pumpkins and potatoes. If you don't want them, I'll take them on to Aunt Benedicta on Saturday."

"Thank you, Annie, I'd love them. We've started a vegie garden, but it's too early yet to get any results. But …why the book?"

"Well, you never know, do you? They're always talking of an invasion from the Japanese; if it happens I'll be ready. It's a Japanese easy phrase book. Ghastly language, awful to learn, always put me to sleep; that's why I brought it with me."

"The life jacket?"

"Oh, that's dead easy. Just in case you take me on the Manly ferry. You know…Scouts' motto 'be prepared' and all that"

"OK. Let's leave the life jacket. I never even thought of taking you on the ferry."

"Thank God for that. I'd hate it. Now, where *are* you hiding your kids?"

"I've been waiting for this." Monica paused dramatically. "They're with Barbara."

"*Barbara*?

"Yes, now a little more respect, please Annie Watson. I now have a live-in maid who helps me in this enormous place and is simply wonderful with the kids."

"Monica, I'm green with envy. How did you manage that? Did Ernest manage to get more of the money you should have received?"

"Not a shilling. No, my good and clever husband, invented some-thing new to do with rifles … I *think* it was rifles; anyway he received a big pay rise and we, for the first time in our lives together, were able to afford to get some help with all this – the house and the kids."

"What's her name? Where did you get her from? Is she any good? Do you and the kids like her?"

"Well, all of that is very simple to answer. Her name is Barbara, Aunt Benedicta selected this one especially for me; I think she's marvellous and, yes, I like her tremendously, so do the kids. She's also a very good worker." Monica stood up. "Come and see."

Monica took Annie's hand and led her quickly into a child's bedroom which looked out over an area of the garden which was totally secluded.

Annie standing at the window saw a young, plump woman with short brown hair, an engaging smile and a turned up comical nose, playing hide and seek with three energetic little children. It appeared to the women watching, that the maid was enjoying herself as much as the children.

"So, that's Barbara, is it?" enquired Annie.

"Certainly is. I think she's wonderful. She loves the kids and is not afraid of work either. Aunt Benedicta rang to ask me how I was getting along with the girl: I said I hoped she'd stay forever."

"Well, you certainly need it with all the work you have to do." Annie commented. "This place is enormous."

Monica laughed. "Yes, it is, but we love it. Come and have a peek at the baby – but quietly, please."

Later having duly inspected the baby; pronouncing him absolutely perfect, Annie was soon back again sitting at the kitchen table with Monica who wanted to know all the family gossip.

"Annie, I was so hoping to be able to get to Penny's wedding; thank you for the invitation. Ben and I were looking forward to it, but Harry decided that he'd arrive ahead of time, so that plan went west.

"But what was it like? Penelope is such a beautiful young woman. Did she look absolutely lovely as a bride? I'm sure she did."

Annie put on her special judicial look. "Well, as a totally *objective* observer – with no personal axe to grind, besides being mother of the bride, Monica – I think she looked breathtaking," Annie replied, then began to laugh.

"She even took me in hand – and believe me, that's not an easy task! I had to endure being told what to wear; she even made me promise to let her decide on the material, colour and style of the dress.

"I was then told what to do, how to have my hair arranged in some fancy beauty salon, then to have that dreadful new lacquer stuff sprayed all over it to make it behave.

"It looked grand – I felt like a duchess – and the damn hair never moved, but it was as stiff as a board. Sam said, as we were dancing, that it was like dancing with a woman with a wooden head." They both laughed companionably.

Monica smiled roguishly. "But you chose what you are wearing today, Annie, didn't you?"

"I see you're in league with Penny. You're laughing at me! Yes, I did and I've got the colours wrong again, haven't I? I thought this would be right. However ..." Annie pulled a comical face, then started to laugh.

"I saw Penny just before I left Bexford; she told me that I looked as if someone had just been sick all over me. As you can imagine, that boosted my ego no end!"

"No, it looks fine, Annie," reassured Monica. "That tailored grey suit you're wearing is superb. Possibly the colour you chose for the blouse could be different. There are such wonderful shops around here; we could go and see what we could find to buy – they have things here that you can't get anywhere else – but you must agree to me choosing the colour. Agreed?"

"Agreed! You're a pet. I'd love it. Why I have no clothes sense, or sense of colour combination, I simply don't know; I always try so hard, and end up looking like a bag woman."

Annie sighed. "However, people in my village are so kind and so used to me, that if I turned up suddenly all smart and stylish, they probably wouldn't know how to cope with me."

"But it must feel a bit lonely without Penny in the house, Annie."

"To be honest, Monica, it does seem odd. I see her often as she only lives at Bexford – near the station; she and George have rented a house there. So, at home, there's only Sam and Billy to look after now."

"Is Billy any better?" Monica knew of Annie's son and his struggles to live a normal life, with a severe cardiac condition.

"Well, much the same really, but he's so looking forward to getting the second scholarship. He won the scholarship for his fees to go to University, thank God, but he also applied for a scholarship to St John's College.

"These are very hard to get. Cousin Ernest wrote a special reference for Billy. We don't know yet but we've hoping he'll get one."

Annie paused, her voice becoming serious. "Monica, you know, Ernest –beside being so famous and so brilliant – is also a wonderful human being, isn't he?"

Monica nodded her agreement. "He certainly is; I'm proud to be related to him, Annie. What he's done for us is unbelievable."

Annie continued. "If Billy does get a scholarship, it'll be easier for him as he'll live on campus, but if he doesn't, then he's going to try travelling there every day."

She picked up another small cup cake. "These are delicious, Monica. With the scholarship, we'll just have to wait and see what happens. He's set his heart on studying at University and worked so hard to achieve this; please God he'll make it.

"But of more interest now is your new neighbourhood where you're now living. This is a very beautiful area of Sydney; I've always loved it; I remember visiting people here with mother, years ago.

"However, Monica, it's also a very exclusive area; they don't really like newcomers. Tell me, how are you really settling in, I mean, getting to know the neighbours and …well … in general … just fitting in? I was a bit concerned that you'd be snubbed as a new-comer - at least until people got to know you."

"Annie, I don't have to pretend with you; it was difficult at first. I knew nobody and no one knew me. "

"Have you met any neighbours, or made new friends?"

"We did at Mass – we usually go to Darlinghurst; we like that Church. We take Barbara with us: she helps us with the kids. We met another girl from St Mary's there, a young girl, called Pamela Scott – she and Barbara were friends at the Orphanage."

"I've met Pamela; a very refined and good girl, I always thought. Does she work close by?"

"Well, reasonably close, Annie, just at Potts Point. That's only a short distance away. It was through her, that we were introduced to her employers, the Parkers – very friendly people. They've invited me to afternoon tea a couple of times.

"We must remember to go there while you're here, you'll like them. Mrs Parker asked me especially to let her meet you." Monica poured more tea for Annie.

"We also met a very dear, elderly, Italian woman, Angelina Falconi, who is very shy, but I did manage to get her to come to tea one day. She was so excessively grateful I felt embarrassed. I feel so sorry for the Italians here in Australia."

"So do I Monica," Annie responded vigorously. "In my own little village, some of my best friends – Italians who have been here for generations – have been interned as *aliens*. I think it's scandalous – they're as Australian as we are."

"Please don't get my husband on the subject of internees, Annie. His best friend at University was a young German lad, from Adelaide. They started together at the same engineering firm all those years ago; suddenly he was whipped off to an internees' camp as an enemy of the state. God help us, poor Heinz wouldn't hurt a fly."

"Oh, Monica," sighed Annie, "this war! Is it ever going to end? Families are torn apart, everything is overturned and now we have to face the horrors of the Japanese. Thank God for the Americans who came to our aid – no one else did. If they don't succeed in the Pacific against the Japanese, we're sunk."

"It's a terrible thought, Annie, especially if you have young children," agreed Monica worriedly. She shook herself and deliberately began a new topic.

"Talking about children, how did you manage to get a few days off from your own family, Annie?"

Annie started to giggle. "Monica, do you remember Dorothy Dwyer? She's your cousin as well as mine."

"You mean the 'Dithering Dotti'?" Monica started laughing, and Annie joined in.

"That's the one! Well, she was in a spot of trouble back at her own house and asked if she could stay with us for a few days. My son Billy thinks she's a scream and even poor Sam thinks she's funny.

"Because of that, I agreed to her coming to take my place for a few days, while I escaped and came to you; then I'll go on to stay with Mother Benedicta, for two days. This is the first little holiday I've had since the kids were born." Annie started to smile.

"When I told the family I was off to the red-light district of Kings Cross for a wicked holiday, they were highly amused. Sam said I'd most probably either change the whole character of the place, or end up as a very successful 'madam' of a high class brothel – he said he thought the second possibility was more likely."

Monica laughed, then putting on a stern face, demanded. "Now, Annie, the truth! How did you manage to get a lift all the way here on an Army truck? No fibs allowed – the whole truth nothing but … etc. etc."

"Oh, dear, I thought I'd got away with it. Where did I go wrong?'

"Well, how come you were talking to Penny at *Bexford* when you came on an army truck?"

"Yes, that was a dead giveaway slip, wasn't it? The trouble is, Monica, the truth is so often boring. I get this urge to embroider it a little."

"The simple truth is, Major Waters, our dear friend from the Convalescent hospital, had a group of young soldiers going to Victoria Barracks this morning and he knew I was coming to see you.

"He also knew, of our dismay, that our old bus had broken down *yet again* and I was stranded. He drove me to Bexford where I saw Penny for a few minutes and the truck picked me up from there on his orders."

"Is that all?"

"There you are. I knew you'd be disappointed. Now, let's go and see these kids and I'll tell them a story that will thrill them to bits, or else give them nightmares for a month."

"No, wait on a minute. As we're telling the truth, now tell me about the book and the life jacket."

"Oh, dear is nothing sacred? Well, the boring truth is that the book is real and I am trying to learn Japanese – while the 'life jacket' is all the apples I could carry from the last of the late summer crop – I was hoping you'd only find that out later. Anyhow, today food is as good as a life jacket, so it really wasn't a complete fib."

The two women laughed happily, and linking arms, moved out to the garden to see the three children and to catch up on all the family gossip.

3

Pamela Scott loved this little park with its benches and trees in the middle of a big city. She enjoyed watching the young girls from the shops and offices rushing over in their lunch hour with their packages of sandwiches.

Pamela listened attentively to their chatter and wished she could join in. Occasionally, some of the girls smiled at her. This made her feel as though she belonged – at least in a little way – to the big, bright, modern, grown-up world of busy and important people.

She reached into her purse and sneaked a little glance at a small mirror there – yes, she had no crumbs on her lips from her lunch. She thought she might leave the apple till later; it was difficult to eat that politely, without a knife of some sort.

Pamela was a moderately tall, slender girl, nearly eighteen years of age, with golden hair which was caught in a clasp behind her neck. She was not beautiful, but a very attractive girl, whose facial structure was such that she would still be a very attractive woman when mere 'prettiness' had long passed away.

Her grey eyes were large and fringed with long lashes while her eyebrows, being a darker shade of gold – almost brown – accentuated the colour of her eyes. Her nose was straight and thin; her mouth beautifully shaped. Her skin was fine and delicately coloured. She had used a soft rose colour for her lipstick but apart from a little face powder, used no other cosmetics.

She was new to the city and, apart from the people in her employer's house and Barbara, her friend from the Orphanage, knew no one else at all.

Pamela felt shy in the company of these city girls, aware that she looked different from them. She knew her clothes were not smart; that they were homemade. They were sensible and modest and made to last; not at all like what the girls she could see in the park, or working in the huge offices in the heart of this big city, wore.

Those girls looked so smart in their fashionable clothes and extremely high heels; Pamela thought she would like to have a pair of shoes like that, but wasn't sure how she'd manage to walk in them. She would've like to ask them how they did it.

The girls also used such clever make-up, too. She would like to know more about make-up – she had attempted to learn from some magazines with little success.

Pamela smiled as she remembered Sister Clare's classes on grooming and make-up – back at the Orphanage – to the senior girls who were about to leave and enter the work-force.

The classes had been hilarious, with Sister reading from an instruction manual, with the girls attempting to follow directions in front of hand-held mirrors. Since coming to the city to work, Pamela, who had a good sense of humour, had come to the sorry conclusion Sister Clare didn't have much idea of make-up either!

Besides looking different from the other girls, Pamela was sadly aware that she had nothing to *talk* about. She didn't know anybody, had never been to dances, or parties and went alone to the Pictures on her days off. She was also shrinkingly aware that *if* she did start talking about the only home she had ever known – a Convent Orphanage – the others would be bored to death, or… worse still, might say cruel things.

Pamela was no fool; she knew that society looked down on anyone from an orphanage; it usually meant you were illegitimate and had been abandoned. Pamela thought this so unfair. Even if it were true, it wasn't the fault of the one abandoned!

However, this awareness, made the girl diffident in the presence to other young girls her age.

Perhaps, she wondered, it might have been easier for her to mix, if Sister Mary Thomas had managed to get an office job for her. She was certainly trained in typing and shorthand, but while waiting for a suitable position, the parlourmaid job had come along so Pamela took it as a chance to start work; she could look for other work herself.

Even though Pamela realised, privately, she had a good job and was not ashamed of doing housework, she guessed that these bright, sophisticated city girls would think a job as a servant, demeaning.

She cringed at the thought that they might actually despise her, while feeling ashamed at the same time *by* the thought. It seemed so disloyal to her employers who were very good, kind people who were very good to her.

A shadow fell on her and the sun was blotted out. Pamela looked up surprised. A very good-looking young man was standing awkwardly in front of her. He was a little taller than she was, had clear, slightly tanned skin, brown eyes which appeared shy and dark hair a little longer than usual. He also sported a thin dark moustache, which hovered over finely modelled lips which in turn revealed beautiful white teeth.

She blushed as she stared at him; he looked like a film star she had seen at the Pictures.

"Excuse me, Miss," the man enquired, his eyes blinking nervously, "do you mind if I sit here beside you while I eat my lunch. I'm on my own too."

Pamela smiled shyly. "Please do, there's plenty of room." She moved to the very end of the bench, as the man sat down, making sure he put the heavy briefcase firmly between his knees.

He opened the grease-proof paper wrapping on his sand-wiches and commented on the weather. After they had discussed the weather and expressed their horror at the state of the war and marvelled at the fact that they both were terrified at the prospect of a Japanese invasion, Lucky thought it time to move in.

"Do you mind if I introduce myself to you? I am Francis Falconi, but my friends call me Lucky. Would you call me that?"

Pamela was confused and touched. She spoke hesitantly, "I would like to call you that, Lucky," she replied. "My name is Pamela Scott. I work as a …"

"Top Secretary to a big and important business man who is fat and horrible with teeth that stick out and who makes you take shorthand at the rate of 300 words a minute," Lucky finished her sentence, laughing.

Pamela looked startled, then laughed merrily; this young man was funny, as well as very nice; handsome too, as well as kind. She hastened to set the record straight.

"No, that's not true. But it *is* true that I am trained in office work. Sister tried hard to get me an office job, but this other job came up as a parlourmaid, so I thought I'd take it while I looked for something better.

"However, I've got to like the people I work for and the cook is a lovely, motherly woman, so I think I'll stay on there. It's only a short way away at the lovely big white house in Lilac Street, Potts Point. So, it's close to the shops and all the other exciting things happening here in the big city."

"You said, 'Sister'? Do you mean your own sister?"

Pamela blushed again. "No, Lucky, I don't have any sister – I wish I did – but I do have a 'capital letter' Sister. You see, I'm from an Orphanage and the Sister I spoke of is a Sister Mary Thomas who has the very hard job of trying to find good places for all of us, when we finish school and our training. She scours the papers, badgers employers and has scouts everywhere trying to make sure we get, not only decent jobs, but with decent people as well."

Pamela was suddenly aware of how much she was telling a stranger about herself – she had been warned by Sister Clare of this. Her brow furrowed; this was dangerous; she must be more prudent – she was in the big city now. "I'm sorry, I'm talking too much and it's boring."

"It's not boring in the slightest. I'm glad you're Catholic; I am too. I'm named after St Francis – you know the one with… animals and … um …er… bare feet." For the moment Lucky couldn't exactly remember who, or what, St Francis was, or did.

He quickly continued: "Which Orphanage did you come from? One close by?"

"No, the big St Mary's Orphanage and Girls' Home at The Junction."

"Oh, that's a big place. I've heard of it; I'd like to see it. I think I've seen the nun in charge of the place in the paper – her photograph, I mean. I think she's something very important."

Pamela's face glowed with delight. "Well, she is to us, anyhow. She's a wonderful woman; we call her 'Mother' and that's exactly what she is, a mother." Pamela looked steadily at the man.

"But, you're right, she *is* actually the Lady Benedicta from a very great family, but," Pamela started to smile, "she's also one of the funniest and most loving women I've ever met."

"How wonderful it is to hear that! I'd love to meet her. I have great respect for nuns and you clearly do as well. That's another thing we have in common. Do you know, my mother goes to Mass every single day and she prays all the time? She has religious pictures all over the house – well, downstairs anyhow.

"I live with my grandfather and my mother. There, you know all about me, now." Lucky laughed.

"Except what you do, Lucky," Pamela remarked, smiling. "It's unusual today to see any man who's not in uniform, so I think you must have a very important job because you are dressed so well and I think it could be something in the Government. Am I close?"

The young man beamed at her. He leant back and pretended to study the young woman closely. "You don't happen by any chance to be a witch, do you? If you are, I can't see any crystal ball."

"You don't mean to tell me I was correct," Pamela laughed incredulously.

"Correct? You're spot on!" Lucky moved closer and whispered. "Pamela, I cannot speak freely about my work as it *is* involved with the Defence Department in the Government – that's why I'm not in uniform – but, yes, it's important and very secret."

Pamela breathed quickly in excitement. "Oh, thank you for telling me; your secret is totally safe with me – I never betray confidences."

Lucky looked quickly at his wrist watch. "Heavens! I've got to dash. I shouldn't have spent so much time here. Look, Pamela we've got to meet again. What days are you off? I'll try to fit my schedule in with yours." Lucky stopped, and looked down, as he twisted his hands in his lap – the picture of embarrassment. He stammered: "That is, if you want to see me again, I mean …"

Pamela hastened to assure him. "Of course I would like to see you again. I don't know anyone in the city. I have Wednesday afternoons off, then all day Friday. I usually try to have my lunch here in the park if the weather is fine and in the arcade over the road there, at the corner, if it's wet.

"Perhaps we'll see each other there another time." She held out her hand. "Good bye Lucky, it was very pleasant meeting you."

Lucky took the white hand and held it gently. "Believe me, Pamela, it was my lucky day meeting you. I'll make sure I see you again." He bent down, lifted the heavy case and hurried away, pausing to wave as he reached the corner and quickly vanished from sight.

4

Mrs Peggy Thompson was a plump, comfortable, pleasant woman in her early fifties with blue eyes and grey hair cut short and tightly permed. Peggy had age wrinkles at both eyes and mouth; her cheeks were rosy and her mouth was wide which showed her teeth as she laughed.

She had been with the Parkers for over twenty years coming there with a young child as a young penniless widow after her husband was killed in a railway accident. She needed work and the only thing she could do was to cook. She owed the Parkers a huge debt of gratitude for giving her a job and agreeing to her keeping the child with her as well.

Little baby Maureen had had a special place in the big kitchen, where Peggy could do her work and look after her child, at the same time.

Peggy had seen the Parker children grow up – three boys and a girl. They had always known Peggy and considered her part of their family – she had always been there.

Of the three boys in the family, two were in the army. They always came first into the kitchen and hugged their 'Second Ma' when they came home on leave – or, at least, they once *did*, until one was killed in France, while the other was now in a Japanese Prisoner of War camp.

Peggy shared with Mary and Tom Parker the anguish of both

tragedies. The remaining boy, John, was a barrister, out on his own now and doing very well. The daughter, Jean, had been a problem for her parents just after she left school, but had settled down quickly; she was now determined to pursue an academic career and was doing a second degree at Sydney University in Geology.

Jean was as fond of Peggy as the boys had been. The young woman often spent time in the kitchen explaining to the cook, what she was studying and why it was so important.

Peggy, secretly, thought it was all nonsense – why would any pretty girl want to waste her life studying rocks? However, she loved Jean and listened intently; trying to understand what on earth it all meant.

To Peggy, Jean was beautiful and should be getting on with her life, getting a good husband and starting a family, not bothering with all this nonsense. Rocks! Who on earth was interested in rocks?

But, perhaps that what girls do now, she thought, sighing; it's a new world. And Jean was a good girl and Peggy had approved highly, when she saw how Jean had come to the support of her parents, when the tragedy of her brothers occurred.

She came home, frequently now – almost every weekend and encouraged Mary, her mother, to go out and to invite people to the house. She also encouraged Peggy to cook exotic things, for special afternoon teas, which she arranged for her mother.

In that way Mrs Parker could not avoid entertaining friends who wanted to be the support she needed, during this awful time of waiting, not knowing whether her prisoner-son was alive or dead.

Peggy was clearing away the afternoon tea things – it being Pamela's afternoon off – and felt grateful for the genuine kindness of her employer. She had insisted that the cook stay and have tea with her, as her husband, Tom, was in the city. They had spoken of the family and then of the new friend the Parkers had made, Monica Jeffrey.

Mary had informed Peggy that Monica was bringing her cousin

to afternoon tea tomorrow, Thursday; Barbara, their new live-in maid would be looking after the children.

Mary Parker had also confided to Peggy that she was looking forward to meeting this particular cousin of Monica's, as she was the daughter of the late Lady Mary Sheridan. And," she confided, smiling, "according to Monica, she was slightly eccentric, but a brilliantly clever lady who had come to the aid of Monica when her mother, the Lady Emily, died.

Peggy knew Monica Jeffrey – she had been a number of times to see Mary Parker. Peggy liked her and thought Monica was a genuine woman with no pretence about her.

Peggy admired the way she managed her children on her own, until she had managed to get decent help with that girl, Barbara – she seemed a nice girl too, and competent as well, according to Monica.

Mary Parker had been delighted when Monica had brought the new baby, Harold, for her to see. The older woman had held the baby in her arms and wept unashamedly, as she remembered her own boys. Monica had wisely let her cry softly, herself remaining totally silent.

Thinking about babies and children, Peggy thought, with sadness, of her own child Maureen. In her love and pride in her employers' daughter's achievements, she tried to imagine what it would have been like if her own Maureen had grown up to be like Jean.

Whenever she thought of her own precious flesh and blood, Peggy's faith in God dropped another notch.

What more could I have done she asked herself repeatedly. I couldn't be with her every moment of the day when she was growing up. How could I introduce her to decent friends?

Why wasn't she like the Parker kids? They had turned out well, why not my Maureen? It's wasn't fair! Why couldn't she have found friends at the Convent school she attended for High School? But, she didn't like them and the girls certainly didn't like her.

Then, that crowd she got in with! God in Heaven help us! Where the hell did she find *them*? Of course, living so close to Kings Cross was difficult for any youngster – it all looked so glamorous; so like those terrible American Pictures – the flashing lights, the huge crowds on the streets, the noise, the music, the cafés; the night-clubs.

Well, it *had* proven too much for her Maureen.

Peggy had noticed the change that had gradually taken place in the last twelve months. She had come to grips with the short skirts, the startling make-up; the 'tarty' look and had to live with the fact that she had moved out of the safety of the Parker's home, into a 'flat' – or, so she said.

Peggy wasn't sure exactly *where* Maureen was living.

She certainly wasn't at the address she'd given her mother – she'd soon found that out!

One night, Peggy was searching the main street of the Cross, looking for her daughter and had finally found her – just getting into a car with three men who were drunk and arguing about who was going to pay!

Peggy had come home a wreck, knowing that it was all over, unless a miracle occurred. She was inconsolable with grief; had cried herself to sleep that night, and several nights following. Her whole life had collapsed; it meant nothing – all she had tried to do for Maureen had been worthless.

This Wednesday evening, as she sat darning stockings waiting for the new maid, Pamela, to return from her half day off, she was pondering the fact that she had not seen Maureen for – how long would it have been? At least two months.

Suddenly there was a scratching at the kitchen door. Peggy started up in alarm, and going to the door, saw through the glass that it was her own daughter.

She rushed to open the door and Maureen almost fell into the room. She clutched at her mother for support. Peggy looked in horror at her child. The eyes were glassy and unfocused, the mouth slack, the make-up streaked across her face and she had a wound in her arm from which blood was weeping.

Peggy brought her child in, put her into the big chair, saw to the arm and managed to stop the bleeding, by binding it tightly with bandages. She made coffee, and forced Maureen to drink it. Slowly, the young woman took notice of her surroundings and attempted to laugh – the resulting horrible, rasping, sound agony to the mother.

"Look where I am! The homing instinct; back home to Mummy!" she mocked. "I didn't know I was coming here! I didn't know where I was going – just wanted to hide."

"Maureen, darling, what've they done to you? Tell me. If there is any way I can help – I'll do anything – please, please let me do it." Peggy held the young woman in her arms. "You're all I've got."

Maureen pushed her away roughly. "You're no good to me unless you can come up with a thousand pounds – pretty bloody quick."

"What!"

"That's what they want. It's what I owe them for the dope."

"Maureen, I've never in my life had that much money. You can have all the savings I've got, but it's only about two hundred altogether."

"Well, get it, then. It might hold them off until I can earn it."

"Earn it? Oh, my God! Maureen let's go away. We'll go up country. It's always easy to get a good job as a cook. They couldn't touch you then. You could start again."

"Are you kidding? Do you want a junkie on your hands? Can't you realise that if I don't get the stuff I'll go insane." She shook her mother off. "If you want to help, get the money and let me go. I could be earning more this night – there's plenty of soldiers about."

At this point, Pamela came home through the kitchen door. She gazed in bewilderment at the figure in the chair, then realised who the poor creature must be.

Peggy was horrified that Pamela had seen her daughter and tried to shield her from view. Pamela however, forestalled her. She went to Maureen's chair and put her hand gently on the arm of the street walker.

"You must be Maureen; I'm Pamela. Your mother's my best friend, and she speaks of you all the time. I'm happy to know you, Maureen." Pamela moved away. "I'm off to bed now so I'll leave you now with your mother."

As Pamela left the room, Peggy went to get her savings from under the stockings in her corset drawer. Returning with the money, she found her daughter crying. "For the love of Christ, keep that kid right away from me; I'll destroy her otherwise."

She stood up and spoke hurriedly: "Got the money? Good. Might see you again, might not." With that, Maureen was through the kitchen door, and gone. Peggy sat at the kitchen table her head in her hands, her eyes squeezed tightly shut.

5

Justice Maurice Bernstein climbed wearily into his chauffeur-driven car and leaned back against the cushions. He was tired... so very tired; it was a relief just to relax his posture after hours sitting rigidly upright, on the Bench.

His eyes closed; he mentally sighed with satisfaction; that wretched seven-week trial was over at last and the obvious villain put where he belonged – for the rest of his natural life.

The judge smiled grimly to himself. How much easier it had been in earlier periods. This murderer had been obviously guilty after the very first hearing, but now with all the endless mitigation for the defendant, owing to his bad upbringing, his poor sense of self-worth, his lack of proper education, his problems with his mother; it seemed to the judge that the only person being forgotten in these modern times, was the victim lying dead in the morgue.

Judge Bernstein hated this new breed called Psychologists: their long winded reports with all those jargon words in the hands of manipulative defence lawyers. He hated Psychologists even more than Psychiatrists; at least, *they* had a medical degree behind them – psychologists, the judge assigned to the same category as sooth-sayers, dubious seers and astrologers.

So many times, during the past trial, he had taken a secret delight in halting the defence in full flight, by demanding that the lawyer explain, to the jury, the meaning in simple words of phrases such as, 'sibling rivalry', 'fixations', 'complexes', 'compulsive behaviours', 'narcissistic tendencies'.

As a consequence, the defence lawyers hated him and were made look fools as they were forced to take a fancy phrase and explain it in simple, everyday terms, which robbed them of the high ground and made them look ridiculous. Many of them, actually, were unable to do as demanded – to the secret amusement of the judge.

The Prosecution, on the other hand, admired him greatly, while the jury members were immensely grateful if he were presiding; he made things comprehensible.

This last case had been a tricky one; the man accused of a very brutal murder – known to the press as 'Simon the Slasher', but to the Judge, as Simon Bayers – was one of those allegedly working for a crime-boss, called Paolo Falconi.

Falconi, the judge knew, was a very powerful King Cross identity who, it was rumoured, had a finger in just about every illegal enterprise in that dangerous, but thriving, sink of iniquity, which at the moment, seemed full of every American on leave from the Pacific area of the war.

It appeared that Falconi was untouchable; every attempt to convict him ended in chaos. The judge had also heard the rumours that Falconi had the support of a good number of police on his payroll.

It was on account of Falconi that Judge Bernstein had asked his chauffeur to wait while he sat in his car pondering his next move.

For the first time in his life, he had received an invitation to drop in and meet Falconi at his house in the city. This was unprecedented; Bernstein was intrigued. As a judge, his life was light years removed from contact with the actual *bosses* of crime, but he was certainly used to dealing with their *associates*; especially their *employees*, in the dock.

Normally, Maurice Bernstein would have thrown away the letter from Falconi without a second thought. However, with the trial of one of Falconi's men – *allegedly hinted* to be one of his men – now completed, he was curious to actually meet a real-life master of crime, face to face.

The Judge was not often subjected to impulsive actions, in fact hardly ever, but besides being, for many years a judge of the criminal court – and, as such, esteemed as a leading member of an august profession – he was also a *human being*.

Maurice Bernstein – the *man* – was simply *curious*.

He decided he'd meet this 'mystery' man – the co-called master of crime. He secretly wonder if he'd be like the 'Chicago characters' they had on the Pictures. Well, he decided he'd have a little adventure: he'd find out!

Having made this decision, Judge Bernstein, innocently, set in motion, a process which then became unstoppable; which would, eventually, result in tremendous suffering and death.

Opening his eyes and giving himself a mental shake, Maurice leaned forward to his long suffering chauffeur.

"Sorry for the wait, John. I've decided at last where I want you to take me." He handed the driver an address printed on a note pad. "Do you know where this is? You do? Good. Apparently we are to enter by the alley door. And, John," the judge lowered his voice, "if I'm not out in thirty minutes, come and get me; I could easily need you. OK?"

The driver, who had been a long time with the judge, understood the message loud and clear. He nodded, the judge thanked him and the car drove off.

6

Paolo Falconi, commonly known as the Falcon, sat at a large desk in an office on the top floor, of his house in Darlinghurst. It was a huge, attractive, Victorian three-storey, brick terrace corner- house, with an alley on one side, which suited the owner very well.

He had had a doorway built into the alley side of the house that led, via an enclosed staircase, right up to the first floor which, with the large attic bedrooms above under the roof, was his own very private domain. His grandson, Lucky, had his own, large flat in the basement, with its separate entrance, while his daughter-in-law, Angelina, lived on the ground floor.

Angelina was a thin, fragile woman with beautiful dark eyes, grey hair, pale, seemingly-bloodless cheeks and a permanent apprehensive expression. She was expected to do the cooking, cleaning and laundry for the Falcon and her own son, but she ate with neither.

There was a dumbwaiter, worked by pulleys, which connected all three separate apartments of the building. When she received word on the intercom they were ready, she used the dumb waiter to send the meals either upwards, or downwards and collected the dirty dishes the same way, after the meals.

She was always in a state of fearful agitation as she never knew *when* either of the two men would actually require their meals. In reality, Angelina, ever since her husband had been murdered, was a nervous wreck; this constant uncertainty added to her mental turmoil.

She seemed to live in a state of perpetual anxiety; her only solace was to sneak off, when it was possible to do so, to the big Catholic Church at Darlinghurst.

This was her only refuge in the nightmare situation in which she existed. Kneeling in the darkened huge, silent church, alone and unnoticed, she felt free from fear; she felt *safe* … she was safe from *them*!

Angelina's devotions had to be hidden and secretive. Her father-in-law, the Falcon, was a notorious atheist who chose every opportunity to mock everything that Angelina believed in. He sneered at her religious pictures and when she, in desperation at his blasphemy, had attempted to hang a crucifix in his apartment, it caused him to fly into a rage.

He immediately took the crucifix and hung it upside down – which caused Angelina to shriek in terror, which made the Falcon laugh uproariously. When safely back in her own section of the house, Angelina, shakily, begged God to destroy the Falcon – he was the devil incarnate.

The man filled her with terror; she trembled whenever he spoke to her. Every moment of her day was spent in trying not to upset him in any way whatsoever.

The Falcon appeared unaffected by Angelina's prayers. He was tall and massively built; his muscular strength, apparent, even now he had passed sixty. His hair was still plentiful, though flecked, attractively, with grey; his eyes still clear, cold and powerful. He read without glasses.

His face had a few wrinkles around the eyes and the lines running down from the nostrils were now more pronounced and were deeper, hinting at his sensuality, but anyone who didn't know him well, would put him in the late forties, or early fifties, at the most.

He was still a handsome man and the stream of women who visited him – via the back stairs – indicated he still was a virile man.

In character, he was close to everything that poor Angelina thought of him. He loved to destroy – it was really the only thing that gave him intense pleasure. This pleasure was greater if it could be against one who was religious, or who contributed to religious enterprises, in any way.

Even in his love-making he was sadistic; he found no pleasure, unless he caused great pain and suffering. In his business dealing – and they were manifold, he was utterly ruthless. He gave commands, expected them to be carried out; if they were not he sent two of his 'boys' to teach a lesson which usually put the recalcitrant into hospital – occasionally into the mortuary.

The Falcon's favourite weapon was the knife, but he had been familiar with guns since childhood. He employed twelve men and kept two muscle men, Tarzan and Jane, as his own personal body-guards. No one even *dared* to snigger at the name of the second guard, who was also an expert with the knife. Jane was well known for his delight in cruelty in his approach to punishment. Everyone feared the Falcon and his associates; this gave him immense personal pleasure.

The Falcon was looking forward to receiving his guest today. He had seen him in the public area of the court and could see him in his mind's eyes as he waited for him: a short, exquisitely dressed, forty-year-old Jewish man, who would be wearing an emerald ring and gold cufflinks. He also knew this judge of the Supreme Court – about whom there had never ever been one hint of corruption in his life – was quite unique.

Falconi looked at the clock; it was time and he was ready. He opened a drawer in his desk, looked briefly in, chuckling silently. He was going to enjoy this; it was going to be entertaining.

7

Falconi waited while the expensively dressed man opposite him at the desk, had taken a sip of the wine pronouncing it excellent.

The judge had explained, politely, that he never drank alcohol in the daytime, and gracefully refused the offer of another glass. As his guest placed the wine glass, still nearly full, back on the desk, the Falcon nodded to his guards, who silently withdrew to another room. He looked intently at his visitor; it was obvious the judge was going to ask why he received an invitation to visit – so the Falcon forestalled him.

"Judge, I asked you to honour me with a call today as you are the Chairman of a Charity Committee having a special Ball and Auction Night, this week – Friday night to be exact."

The Judge looked surprised; his eyebrows rose. What on earth has that to do with Falconi? What was this slippery chap up to? Surely he wasn't about to give a donation – that would be a first! From what he'd heard, he *took* 'donations', he didn't give them!

"Yes, that's true." He replied briefly.

"It's a Charity affair, I know. I asked you here today, as I want to inform you *which* Charity the proceeds will benefit." The Judge spluttered; this was outrageous!

"What? You can't do that! It has already been decided by the committee."

"Nevertheless, you will convince them to change their mind.

It will be the one that I recommend. And," the Falcon continued, ignoring the spluttering protests from his visitor, "that will be St Mary's Orphanage and Girls' Home at The Junction."

"But *why* that Charity? Have you gone suddenly religious or something?"

The Falcon swore blasphemously. "Perish the sodding thought. You mind your own business about my reasons. I'll handle things the way I want them done. You have to do just exactly what I tell you to do …or else."

"Or *else?*" The Judge was incensed. He started to rise from his chair; he'd made a mistake; he should never have come to this place. "You would not dare to threaten me, would you, Falconi? Why on earth *should* I change the decision the committee has made?"

"Well, you needn't, if you don't want to. I'm quite indifferent as to which charity actually gets the money. If you don't like that idea, you could just write a cheque for two thousand pounds, payable to me."

The Falcon spoke calmly and cut the end off a cigar. He did not look up, nor offer a cigar to his visitor. The judge had had enough; he stood up – he would leave immediately.

"You must be out of your mind, Falconi! Why, on earth, should I write a cheque to you for that amount, or for *any* amount?" The Judge was aware that something was terribly wrong somewhere; he'd fallen into some kind of trap.

"What's going on, Falconi?"

"You will do as you're told, as it's simply what you owe me."

"*Owe* you? What for?"

"For not revealing to the press that you – a pillar of society and endlessly in the society pages of the press, besides being a Judge of the Supreme Court, the terror of villains in the dock – are in the habit of visiting a bordello.

"I have some very entertaining pictures here you might like to see." The Judge stood by his chair, his face reflecting his bewildered fury, as the Falcon opened a drawer in his desk and took out a number of lurid pictures.

"I'll have you in court for this slander, Falconi; it's a complete lie and you know it."

"Oh, I admit that freely, but spare a look at the photos, Judge. Anyone seeing those photos in the newspapers would swear that the little chap, without his clothes on, was you, wouldn't they?" The Judge looked at the photos and recoiled with horror. It was true, there was a definite resemblance.

He understood, now, he was going to be blackmailed and that this was not a sudden unpremeditated affair. His hand began to tremble.

"Why are you doing this, Falconi?"

"You might remember that today you sentenced one of my men to life imprisonment. I sent you word not to do that; you disobeyed. This is your punishment." Falconi puffed contentedly on his cigar.

"Next time you have a man of mine in front of the Bench, you will remember the consequences, if you do not let him off leniently."

"I refuse utterly to do what you demand. No one who knows me would believe those disgusting pictures are of me."

"Your wife is that broad-minded is she? That's nice. No marriage problems? Perhaps she'll overlook the little indiscretion, when she sees the photos in the newspapers. Her friends will have a good laugh though, won't they?" The Falcon laughed quietly, studying the photos closely.

"Damn you, damn you, damn you ... This is intimidation, fraud and blackmail! How dare you do such a thing!" the Judge was nearly incoherent in his fury. After all his years on the bench dealing with every evil crime on the books, he had been taken in like a novice.

"Oh, I think I will be damned; it doesn't bother me. I think I'd be happier *down* there than *up* there with the likes of people such as you." The Falcon paused and gestured with his hand.

"Go away, you little man; I eat little men like you for breakfast."

He yawned. "You have until eight o'clock tonight to make up your mind: either a cheque for two thousand pounds payable to me, or else persuade the committee to make the charity proceeds out to St Mary's Orphanage and Girls' Home at The Junction. I've heard that's the amount they expect to make from this function.

'I'll handle it from that moment on. All you have to do is convince the two other committee members and then call me.

"It would be advisable to call me tonight *before* eight and tell me if you've done what I said; if you do not call before eight, it will still be in time for me to send the pictures for the morning papers.

"Now, do go away little man! You bore me." Falconi pressed the bell under his foot and the two guards returned as silently as they had left.

His honour, Justice Maurice Bernstein, moved from the chair he had been holding, and stumbled from the room.

After he had gone, the Falcon laughed contentedly; it had all gone according to plan. His henchman laughed with him, not knowing what was amusing the boss – that didn't matter; they had learned early on, in the service of this man – it was foolish not to do so!

8

Unknown to the Falcon, Angelina had heard every word he had spoken to the Judge.

She'd been cleaning the oven of her stove downstairs and had forgotten that the door to the dumbwaiter, had been accidentally left open; it was, usually, always closed tight.

To her surprise, she had heard voices coming from upstairs and going close to the opening in the wall, Angelina discovered that the gap in the wall for the dumbwaiter, acted as a sounding board – she'd never noticed that before, or if she had, she had paid no notice to the voices above her.

Holding her breath, Angelina listened in horror to the plan of the robbery – for it was instantly clear to her that the Falcon intended to keep the proceeds of the function: no charity would ever receive a penny from him!

She was then further alarmed to hear the *name* of the place, that was to be robbed. He was going to rob *that* Orphanage! To add to her terror and grief, it wasn't long after this that she heard the Falcon speak on the phone to the convent at the Orphanage.

She almost shrieked, when she heard him ask for a Sister Mary Josepha. In her fright, Angelina knees gave way; she sank to the floor. She shoved her apron into her mouth to stop her screaming in anguish.

When she recovered a little, she crossed herself rapidly and began praying out aloud in Italian. *He's found out!* After all the years! I've kept her safe from him! Oh God, help me! He must now know where she is! She's no longer safe! Her life's in danger! He'll kill her, as he killed her father.

Dear God in Heaven; Holy Virgin Mary, what *can* I do? *He'll kill her!*

9

At St Mary's Orphanage and Girls' Home, Sister Mary Josepha was working in her office on the endless accounts, preparing the totals to be checked by her assistant, Sister Mary Margaret.

Josepha was meticulous in everything she did, carefully checking again and again, that every single item had been properly classified. The lists of amounts; the names and addresses of donors, were ready; she could now take them to the two girls next door. They would type the little 'thank-you' notes, and include a small holy card, or some Scripture verse the Sisters had printed.

Before she left the office, Josepha adjusted carefully the wide, heavy sleeves of her black habit, to their original position and slightly straightened the stiff coif that surrounded her face and formed a large starched guimp across her chest.

As she rose from her chair to go to the typists, her full and heavy skirts, finely pleated, fell into folds to her shoes, while she gave an automatic tug to her leather belt from which hung her large rosary beads and adjusted the large crucifix which was placed in the centre of her belt – it had slipped a little from being so long at her desk.

She was about to leave the room, when a young girl from the senior school hurried in.

"Excuse me, Sister Josepha, but Mother Benedicta asked me to tell you that you are wanted on the telephone. Mother said it was urgent."

For a moment the nun stared at the child. Recollecting herself, she thanked the girl courteously, her face perplexed. Who on earth could be asking to speak to *her*? It *must* be about one of the girls – possibly one of them is in some trouble … but … they wouldn't ask for *me*: I don't have much to do with them, here in this section – they don't really know me at all.

Well, whoever it was, she had to face it. It could be a bank problem.

She hurried to the community telephone which was in a small alcove near the Superior's office, her usually serene face troubled.

Picking up the receiver she heard a man's voice demanding to know if she were there. At the sound of the voice, Sister Josepha began trembling.

That voice! No, never again! *She would never ever forget that voice!* Her hand began to shake uncontrollably; she had to use her other hand to steady the receiver.

After what seemed an age, she summonsed up enough courage to whisper. "Yes." The voice went on – giving her no chance of replying.

"Listen and I'll tell you what you have to do. Make sure you remember this name: *The Acme Messenger Service*; it's the one that will be picking up the proceeds from a Charity Ball, Friday night. A member of the charity committee will be calling on you soon, to collect the bag for the money – give them the bag you usually use and have it tagged with the Orphanage name. You'll get the bag back Saturday morning.

"I'll repeat the name: *The Acme Messenger Service*. Phone the Charity Committee, this is the number; write it down." The Falcon repeated the numbers slowly, "and tell them the name of the collectors.

"I don't need to remind you to do exactly as you're told. *I know where you are now.* You, and your precious mother, thought you'd fooled me – you are both simpering, drooling, idiots. You'll do whatever I order you to do, without questioning me. Let me remind you of the little accident your father had ..."

A long chilling silence followed, then the voice went on: "And then, of course, there's your mother – the mad one ... perhaps your mother's face would be all the better for a little face-lift – she's grown quite ugly now, you know; I'll think about it ..."

There was a moment's silence, then came a quiet, mocking laugh and the line went dead.

Sister Josepha stood as though turned to marble, the receiver still in her hand. Ever since she'd escaped from the monster and found a refuge – with the added safety of a new name – she had been secretly dreading that, one day... one day... she would again hear that terrifying voice – the voice of a killer – which had always reduced her to a quivering wreck.

She'd always known that one day this would come; no one had ever outwitted the Falcon. He would crush her as he had his own son – her own beloved Babbo.

Dear God, she prayed, what about my mother? He'll cut her to ribbons if I don't do as he says – whatever it means.

Josepha's mind was in turmoil, tyring to understand what she had to do. Who on earth is this committee member she has to ring? And what on earth is the Acme Messenger Service and what does this have to do with us here? God have mercy... *guide* me; I don't know what I am to do.

The Superior of St Mary's, Mother Benedicta, came bustling down the corridor, talking non-stop as usual, to a group of senior girls, who were giggling helplessly, when she caught sight of Josepha. She smilingly motioned the girls away, and went to the younger nun, her plump, mobile, very expressive face, now troubled and full of concern.

The middle-aged Superior was short and dumpty; her veil and guimp seemed perpetually askew, but as the girls and her colleagues well knew, she was a compassionate and loving woman. Her eyes missed nothing; one look at Josepha's face, and she knew there was trouble.

She reached up and put her arm around the taller, younger nun.

"Sister, what is it? You're not well; your face is as white as your coif. Come into my office. Come and sit down for a bit … Are you ill?" The older nun realised that the younger woman was trembling. Josepha shuddered violently then, with a tremendous effort, tried to smile.

She carefully replaced the receiver, managing to say shakily: "A little attack, Mother. Not important in the least. Thank you, but there's no need for any fuss. I'll just get back to my work – there's a load of work waiting to be done; I'll be all right now. Thank you, Mother."

She hurried away, leaving the Superior with worry lines forming on her forehead. What on earth could be the problem? Josepha's never like that; always reserved, polite and courteous, never emotional, yet she was white as parchment and was actually *trembling*.

Something serious has happened. Are her parents still living, I wonder? Perhaps one is seriously ill; but if that's the case, why wouldn't she have told me – the other Sisters would have done so.

Mother Benedicta went slowly to her own office. She was puzzled. In the fifteen years Josepha had been at St Mary's there had never ever been any problems with her.

Benedicta rubbed her nose vexedly. When she came to think of it, Josepha has never had any visitors either – the whole family must be dead, or … could it be that they have disowned her, for entering the convent? Good God, Benedicta had known of that to happen several times, in her life as a nun.

She'd have to ask Sister Mary Michael about Josepha – she would know her better; she would be with her more.

The older woman's face crumpled in vexation. Oh, she cried in exasperation, I don't have enough time to be with the nuns who need me; I don't know them well enough, through and through, as I should. She thumped the mantelpiece in her office in exasperation. *There's always girls – big and small – who demand my attention; I simply don't have enough time!*

There was a knock at her door and a young voice called out the shorthand method they used to ask for a blessing: "Benedicite, Mother," and Benedicta quickly re-arranged her face, smiled, and replied: "Deus. Come in Sister Clare. I'm free now. What horrors are you going to tell me now?"

The young nun laughed and gave her report on the senior girls to her Superior. Gradually, Mother Benedicta's brow cleared. *Well, some things actually do turn out well,* she thought with gratitude, as Sister Clare left the room.

Soon after, however, her plump, pleasant face was puckered again in anxiety over Sister Josepha. With her half glasses slipping down her nose as usual, she rubbed her nose vigorously and … suddenly she stood perfectly still and quickly crossed herself.

She shuddered. *Something is dreadfully wrong – or, about to go wrong – something evil, I know it! An evil angel has just passed over this house!*

10

Two hours later, Sister Mary Josepha made the phone call to the Chairman of the organizing committee for the Charity Ball; she discovered he was a Judge Maurice Bernstein.

She informed him that the proceeds would be collected by a company called the 'Acme Messenger Service' and the self-locking bag for the money would be available from the Sister at the gate of the Orphanage, whenever it suited a member of the committee to collect it.

The Judge grimaced to himself as he listened to the instructions from the nun. The Falcon had not wasted any time in his plan – he had guessed correctly that the judge had no other choice but to agree.

The press would crucify him if those photos were printed – they already called him 'the self-righteous hanging judge'. He thought grimly that the Falcon had won this round, but he promised himself that next time it would be his turn!

He forced himself to concentrate on the details being told him by the nun, and then mystified Sister Josepha completely, by congratulating her on the sudden decision by the committee to choose her Orphanage, as the Charity for the function, instead of another, they had been considering.

Not knowing what on earth he was talking about, Sister Josepha thanked him courteously and replaced the receiver.

With a quaking sensation, the nun realised that whatever was going on, she had, as ordered by the monster, set the whole thing irretrievably in motion; there could be no turning back now, wherever it led and whatever sin it had involved her in. Should she have given in to the threats?

Would that man have done what he threatened? *Yes, yes, yes, he would!* He had murdered *his own son!* He was capable of doing anything! The nun trembled. I have now involved myself in a terrible lie; there could be terrible consequences through doing that. Perhaps other people would die; I would be to blame!

Oh. God, please God, don't desert me!

The nun felt nauseous and fighting desperately against the desire to vomit, hurried to the Chapel instead. For the next hour she was on her knees, her head nearly touching the floor, her mind in anguish.

11

Returning from the park, Lucky delivered the protection money to his grandfather. He gave the usual report, adding that he had no real trouble – that greasy takeaway shop owner had almost split himself trying to be polite and helpful.

The Falcon grunted. He noted the amount Lucky had totalled and was pleased. Perhaps, now might be the time to act. He had to move Lucky up higher; he had to learn the whole business – there's no one else now...it *has* to be him.

The Falcon made meaningless vague murmurs of agreement, as he listened to Lucky's voice, while he thought of his next move in relation to his grandson.

"Sit down, Lucky," he suddenly ordered, motioning the two guards to leave.

After Lucky sat in front of the desk, the Falcon studied him closely. He was glad the boy had taken after him; he was good looking: – a strong, handsome face with regular features and with all this baloney about internees, not *too Italian*-looking for his own safety. The eyes were good and his eyebrows well shaped. His lips were full and hinted at sensuality – that was good; it would attract the girls – the teeth were good – it had been well worth all that money he had spent on that filthy dentist – he had dealt with him afterwards – *he'd* never work again, with seven fingers missing – the drivelling slob.

Looks were very important; Alberto had never understood that.

Paolo Falconi sighed; it was a pity that he had to get rid of Alberto – it would have been nice to hand over the whole business to his son; it had a feeling of immortality about it – passing the business on, from one generation to the next, as his own father had done to him.

Ah well, he reasoned, no use lamenting what can't be fixed! There was some satisfaction in the knowledge the grandson was a carbon copy of himself when he was his age. He'd been a good apprentice so far, but the Falcon knew he must test him to make sure of him completely.

He has to be able to cope with everything *without a scruple* – otherwise he would be useless. The Falcon had already decided on a plan and thought this was the right time to put it into action.

Yes, the timing was right; this would be the right *kind* of test, not just for Lucky, but for the boy's mother as well; it would keep her in line, just in case she started getting any ideas … Yes, it was *exactly* right!

He had always been secretly concerned about Angelina: had he allowed her to have too much influence over the boy growing up? Well, we'll soon find out. His mouth was grim.

Lucky started to become anxious. Was something wrong? He looked intently at his grandfather. "Nonno, is anything the matter? Do you want me to do anything differently?"

The Falcon gave one of his rare smiles. "No, no, Lucky, I'm very pleased with you. I'm just wondering where I'm going to use you next. You've been on the protection racket for a good while now; it's time you had a change. I want you to do more in the recruiting line for the brothels – we need more *young* girls. Sarah was telling me that the customers are demanding that the girls be younger and younger – you know, fresh-faced kids… that kind of look."

"Excuse me, Nonno, for interrupting, but I've been thinking of that, and I've been looking around. Just today, I found a girl – Pamela Scott her name is – about sixteen or seventeen, I think, who's from an Orphanage and she's working as a maid in Potts Point. I struck up a conversation and I arranged to meet her on her next day off."

"An Orphanage?" The Falcon asked quickly. "Which one by any chance?"

"The one at The Junction. I think it's called St Mary's Orphanage and Girls' Home."

There followed a period of complete silence in the room. Paolo Falconi had received an unpleasant shock, which left him feeling slightly queasy. He was violently anti-religion in all its forms, but was wildly superstitious. He quickly crossed his fingers behind his back.

This news from Lucky was a weird coincidence; he didn't really like coincidences – they were *unlucky*. Could he cancel this robbery, he wondered? No, it's too late now to change things; he'd just have to chance it. And, Bloody Hell! Lucky would have to know *now* as he would be playing a major part in the robbery.

He struggled with himself and succeeded in adopting a nonchalant tone.

"Well, well! It's about that very place that I want to speak to you. On Friday night you will go to the Sydney Town Hall, at exactly half past eleven o'clock to the room at the back of the stage. You will be dressed in a Messenger's Uniform – get one from Sarah, she has several – and you'll collect the proceeds of the Charity, which will be in a special locked bag. You'll give a proper receipt – here's the book to use – and sign your name that you've received the money. Your name will be Anthony Moran, and you will have a driving licence in that name, to prove your identity.

"You will sign as Anthony Moran, then taking the bag, you'll bring it here to me. I shall be waiting to receive it. Next morning – that is, on Saturday – you will drive to The Junction and deliver the bag to St Mary's Orphanage, leaving it with the Sister at the gate. You will, of course, use the little grey van. On the sides of the van will be painted, professionally, the words: Acme Messenger Service – it is being done now, as we speak. You will be the messenger of that company for that night. Is that clear?"

"If I am pulled up by the police?"

"You are who your licence says you are and you work in the munitions factory at Glebe – you know the one – but work as a Messenger at night, to help out with expenses; you have three children and a sick wife. The address on your licence will be in Glebe. If they do any checking they'll find there is an Anthony Moran and that he does work at that munition factory there at Glebe."

Lucky chuckled. "A wonderful plan, Nonno! So now I'm a family man!" He smiled happily. "I'll be happy to do it. Now, about this afternoon, any orders? If you don't have anything for me to do, I'd like to spend some time at the gym – I know I'm in good shape, but I'd like to keep it that way – safer for me."

"Go ahead, have a good session in the gym. Very important. I have great hopes for you Lucky. There is just one little thing …"

"Anything, Nonno. You tell me, I'll do it – no questions asked."

The Falcon's face changed; he shifted his position, sitting up rigidly straight; his voice now cold, his eyes piercing… he spoke slowly and deliberately: "I'll hold you to that." He paused, and stared into the depths of Lucky's eyes. "There is one thing missing – that's holding me back about you."

Lucky was alarmed. He spoke urgently.

"What? Tell me. If there's anything lacking, I need to know."

"I want you to kill someone for me." As he heard these words, coldly spoken, Lucky felt his stomach contract.

It was the very last thing he had expected.

He was suddenly frightened – he had not bargained for this. He struggled frantically to control his face – the Falcon missed nothing – he had to appear as if it were of no special consequence.

With great difficulty, he tried to put on his cynical 'Movie' look – as he called it in his mind, using the new 'American' name for the Pictures – of the Chicago gangster; he even attempted to speak, cynically, out of the corner of his mouth.

"Consider it done. Anyone special?"

The Falcon was aware of the pretence going on before his eyes, but keeping his eyes fixed unwaveringly on his grandson, he continued in the same slow, unemotional voice.

"Well, not *special* … but … *different*, anyhow. You see, I want you to kill a nun from St Mary's Orphanage."

Lucky's jaw actually dropped in his astonishment. Try as he could to control his features, he failed to hide his alarm! A *nun*!

His imitation of an American gangster disappeared – for a moment, he was just a frightened young man. He almost forgot himself and went to cross himself – as his mother would have done.

He shivered in his fright. God help him, if he had done that! He remembered fearfully what had happened to Babbo, his father.

"Nonno! What? Why? I don't understand."

The Falcon's cold voice was like steel as he answered: "You said, 'no questions asked'; this is my test of you: to do exactly as you are told to do. Do this and I will know that I can trust you completely and utterly. Pass this test, and you are ready for the big time."

Lucky tried desperately to repair the impression he had given. "Well, I'm sorry I asked those questions, Nonno, but it was a bit of a shock, you'll agree." Lucky relaxed his posture, then took out a cigarette willing his fingers to stop trembling – to all appearances, the phoney American Movie gangster persona was back in control of everything. He took a deep breath to control his voice.

"Of course, I'll do it. When do you want it done?"

"I was thinking this weekend, amid the whole chaos that will ensue over the missing money, but that might not be possible. Let us say, within the next ten days. Remember the success of the operation involves 'quickly in, quickly out and away' before anyone recovers from the shock."

The Falcon took from a drawer on his right a drawing of the Chapel. "Come round to this side of the desk, Lucky. I want you to be familiar with the layout. Then you'd better check out the place within the next couple of days."

Lucky felt slightly sick in the stomach as he went around the desk. He then studied the plan, as his grandfather talked, calming himself by immersing himself in the details of the building, where the killing was to take place.

One floor down, Angelina knelt at the dumb-waiter, the door open, listening as her eyes grew enormous in her horror. She could hardly believe her ears. Those two devils upstairs were calmly planning to murder an innocent nun, and in *that particular convent!*

Once again Angelina slid to the floor clutching the little crucifix she wore around her neck. Her mind – amid the chaos of terror that gripped her – was telling her: *Listen!* Listen carefully to the plans! Learn what these two evil ones are planning. *Listen!* – You might be able to stop them! Putting her head right inside the dumb waiter, Angelina heard the Falcon's voice continue:

"See, the Chapel backs onto the main road and has a door which opens onto the street. That is the public section of the Chapel for lay people who want to go to their ridiculous services.

"There are three steps up from the main door, to the small area set aside for these people. You will be able to see the nuns clearly in their choir stalls through a large grill, which blocks off the public part of the Chapel, from the nuns' part.

"The public area is very small; it has about three short pews and then the grill, so you'll be fairly close to the nuns – you will see them easily. I have discovered that they are in the Chapel several times during the day – the lot of them, I mean – so perhaps an afternoon might be a good time. There is a service at half past four o'clock – it's called Vespers."

The Falcon put his head back and actually laughed aloud with satisfaction, his white teeth gleaming. "That means 'evening' – well, it'll mean evening for one of the black crows surely enough! Seriously though, I think that's a good time; there'll only be about six other people in the public Chapel.

"Kneel at the back, use an army issue gun – they make a hell of a racket, that'll shock them stupid – and once you've fired the shot at whichever one you chose – remember, it doesn't matter to me which one it is – get the hell out as quickly as you can.

"Act totally naturally when it's over, then no one suspects you – just merge into the largest crowd you can find. Is all that clear?"

"Perfectly." The Falcon noticed the lack of enthusiasm.

"Do you have any hesitation about the job? Tell me now, Lucky. If you do have any stupid, superstitious, scruples about it, you are of no use to me. You can stay on the protection racket for the rest of your days."

Lucky was aware of a slight perspiration breaking out on his upper lip. He knew he had to overcome this or he'd be in big trouble. The Falcon would not stand for any weakness. Yet, how could you just shoot a harmless nun? They might be ridiculous, but they do all the jobs no one else wants to do and they look after all the illegitimate brats off the streets.

He thought miserably: they look after people like *Pamela*. She most probably loves them.

But, Lucky's thoughts were surging rapidly through his mind: *this* is what's really important. This time it's either me or the losers and I *won't* be one of the losers, whatever the cost.

What's the big deal, he rationalised; there's plenty more girls like Pamela and it was unlikely she would ever know, anyhow. What's one nun's life in the face of the Falcon's contempt if he refused! And, possibly... not *only* contempt! Lucky cringed mentally, remembering Babbo.

He only remembered him vaguely – he had been eliminated when Lucky was very young, but he still *did* remember him and he had loved him. He remembered also the mystery of his sister, Anna. He had loved her as well, but she, too, had disappeared ... never spoken of again!

Everyone he'd ever loved had disappeared... ... No way! ...

There was no way he could dare cross the Falcon! Whatever it cost, he *must* do whatever he was asked to do.

Lucky looked up and, with a tremendous effort, kept his eyes fixed, unwavering, on his grandfather.

"I'll do it Nonno. You'll be proud of me; I won't let you down."

After a searching glance at the young man, the Falcon appeared satisfied. "Right then, off you go to the gym. Don't forget to get that uniform for Friday night." He waved his hand in dismissal and pressed the bell for his henchmen to return. The interview was over.

***

One floor down, Angelina pressed the tea towel to her eyes. What can I do, dear God what can I do? Her thoughts flew to the young girl, 'Pamela something'. She remembered that nice woman, Monica Jeffrey, talking about her: a friend of their own maid, she had said. And … dear God, that young girl, Pamela, is from the *same* Orphanage as well! *What is going on?* Why is 'him upstairs' doing all this to *that* place? The robbery, the murder … *all concentrated on the same place*. Not content with robbery and murder, they were obviously planning now, to ruin the young girl, Pamela.

Angelina rocked backwards and forwards in her anguish.

Is there no end to their evil, she asked herself distractedly? Could I warn the girl? She'd laugh at me! Why should she believe me? And how *can* I warn the poor girl? She's just out of the Orphanage… she won't stand a chance with men like these two.

The *Police*? From what she'd heard they're on the payroll of the Falcon. She can't go there! What could she tell them anyhow? She'd heard something in the dumb waiter? They'd speak soothingly to her; they'd think her mad!

Angelina actually struck her head against the wall in her distress, and chewed desperately on the tea towel, which she had stuffed in her mouth – she was very close to hysteria and was terrified she'd suddenly scream. She knew if she once started she would be unable to stop!

12

Monica Jeffrey led her cousin, Annie Watson, on a tour of her beautiful garden at her new home. Annie was in her element. Back in her own village, her life revolved around the orchard, her flower garden and the big vegetable garden she and her son worked.

To her delight, she found that Monica's husband was an avid gardener as well; his vegetable garden was huge and would be very productive in time. Annie expressed her delight at this unaffectedly, for although both she and Monica belonged to an ancient and titled family, they were not wealthy; in fact Annie was a poor woman.

Monica and her family lived in a beautiful house, in an exclusive suburb, but that was due entirely to the unexpected inheritance from Monica's mother. The financial situation of both families meant that they needed a vegetable garden, not just for the war effort, but to cut down expenses, in order to survive.

"It's great Monica. You and Ben have done a wonderful job in such a short time."

"Annie," Monica explained, "It really is a joint effort. I try to do the watering and some of the weeding, but with the kids and all the laundry, I never had much time before. Now with Barbara's here to help with the house work, I'm trying to spend more time out here in the garden. Ben works so hard all week I want to do what I can during the weekdays, to help him out."

"You're a good wife and mother, Monica," Annie declared. "You know my feelings about the pampered dolls who think their hands will be ruined, if they dare get a bit of dirt on them." Annie paused and jabbed another bobby pin in her hair.

"I can't stand those pathetic women, who sit around doing nothing all day. Some women think painting their long nails that revolting scarlet red – it always makes me think of blood – is enough work for one day!"

Annie looked with interest at the vegetables and picked up a handful of soil. "This is good soil; you'll be able to grow such vegetables! Our soil is fairly good, but we need a fair amount of manure for the orchard. Sam's been fortunate in getting some loads of that, free, from the local dairy, for both the orchard and the gardens."

Annie's sharp eyes were suddenly drawn to the front of the place. "Monica, is that woman calling you?"

Monica looked around and waved. "Goodness, it's that Italian woman, Angelina, I was telling you about, Annie. I wonder what she wants; she's never been here without warning before."

Both women moved towards the front of the garden and Monica welcomed Angelina. The Italian woman appeared very nervous and stammered something about being in the vicinity; she wondered …

"If you could call and see us," Monica kindly finished the rambling sentence. "Of course you can at any time. Come on into the house and we can have a cup of tea together."

Monica turned to Annie. "Annie, I'd like you to meet a friend of mine, Mrs Falconi. Angelina, this is my cousin, Mrs Annie Watson. If you call her Annie, then she can call you Angelina then, we can forget the formality and just be friends together."

Laughing gently, Monica took the older woman's arm and led her back into the house. Annie, following behind, wondered why Angelina was so obviously frightened; surely it couldn't be of them.

Was it just natural shyness, or something else? It *must* be something else – has she come to confide something serious to

Monica? I could be in the way. If that's seems the case, I'll make myself scarce – I'll go and play with the kids.

Angelina smiled a lot and docilely accepted a cup of tea and answered the questions that Monica and Annie asked to put the woman at her ease.

Annie then, from her long experience in village life, asked about the woman's children – that usually was a good way to begin any conversation with a woman. The response was alarming. The woman began to tremble.

"Dead, all dead," Angelina cried agitatedly. "Husband dead, daughter dead, son dead." Monica was shocked and uttered consoling noises, while Annie was studying the woman closely. Something's wrong with what the woman had said; that's *not* the truth she decided. *Why* is she saying that? Does she *wish* them dead? Would she prefer that they were dead? God forbid! But … if she does, then *why*? Annie decided to risk it.

"But they're not really dead, are they, Angelina," she asked softly. The woman looked at Annie with something akin to terror. She stood up quickly, in her agitation dropping the cup she was holding. "I must go. Sorry, I make mistake coming here… Look, what I do? Forgive, sorry, please." Annie stood up, and took the woman's hand.

"Angelina, you came here to tell Monica something, didn't you?"

"I … no … yes … I must go. I don't know what to do. I afraid… He'll find out I've gone out of house. I'm frightened. He'll know …"

"*Who* will find out?" Annie persisted. The woman pulled her hand free, grabbed her purse and backed away from the table. She whispered something as she turned swiftly and hurried from the house into the garden. She was out the gate and actually running, by the time she reached the street.

Monica stood staring. "What on earth? Is she mad, do your think? Did you catch what she said as she was leaving, Annie."

Annie's face was troubled. "I think she said: 'the Falcon,' but what that means I have no idea. But, one thing is clear. The woman is terrified out of her mind about something, that's about to happen."

The sun suddenly was hidden by clouds. Annie shivered. "Someone has just walked over my grave," she murmured darkly, "there's evil afoot, Monica, and somehow or other, I have a horrible feeling, willy-nilly, we're involved in it."

13

Lucky travelled by tram to the gym. He paid his fare as the conductor swung himself along the precarious foot-rail, which ran each side of the tramcar, then wedged himself in the doorway, as he took the money and gave out the tickets.

There was one seat left in the small compartment. Lucky sat down and stared moodily at the other passengers. He was not in a good mood. Even the woman opposite him with a ridiculous little hat with feathers at one side, irritated him. He scowled at her; she averted her eyes quickly.

After he had left the Falcon, Lucky had wondered if his mother's religious superstitions had had more effect on him, than he had realised. Otherwise, why would he be so concerned about the job ahead? It was only a nun; she was just an ordinary dame, even if she was dressed up in pretty fancy clothes, so why was there a problem? He was confused and he hated being confused – he liked things black and white; you knew where you were then.

It wasn't as if he was morally shocked and didn't know the extent of his grandfather's activities. He knew of the stand-over tactics, the brothels, the crooked doctors he employed, the abortionists, the police on his payroll, the dope and the endless girls of all ages he used. He knew there were killings, but previously they had never involved *him* – they were impersonal, side-issues; jobs that concerned other people, on Nonno's payroll – never *him*.

Money poured into his grandfather's purse and Lucky knew the Falcon was one of the top three bosses who virtually ran the entire Kings Cross red-light district. Lucky was not a fool; he knew full well that you didn't get to that position by being a goody-two-shoes.

He shrugged mentally. I suppose, he reasoned, it's just nerves. I've never actually killed anyone outright before. I've wounded enough, but I've never actually killed them. There was something horribly *final* about that thought; it was the final snuffing out of a life of a living, breathing, human-being.

Lucky held his breath as he thought of the actual kill; would he be able to go through with it when the time came?

He had no option; he *had* to do it! He found himself shivering, but as he experienced that physical reaction, he thought what his mother would say about *that*. She would immediately say an evil angel had just passed over him. He grimaced at the thought.

Get your mind on to something else. A good work-out at the gym might do the trick; a lot of hard, tiring work, lots of sweat, a long hot, then cold, shower. That's the answer; he'd be as right as rain after that.

The tram shuddered to a halt. Some of the passengers were getting out. The middle-aged woman opposite Lucky leant over him, as she was leaving, and, before he could react, had put into his top pocket, *a White Feather*.

Lucky stared at the feather in stunned disbelief – he had never ever had that shameful thing happen before. Never! For a moment he sat shocked; then recovered, just as the tram began to move. He leapt to his feet in fury, and jumped from the moving tram, ignoring the shouts of warning from the conductor and the honking of cars.

He reached the other side of the street safely and saw in the distance the woman who had dared to denounce him, publicly, as a *coward* by giving him the White Feather!

By God, he'd make her pay for that! That stupid hat with the feathers; it was easy following the bitch; he'd give her *feathers*!

14

Mrs Eileen Hodges, a widow, proudly called herself a patriot. She was on every committee that concerned the war, working fearlessly and tirelessly, for each money-raising function, that would aid the victory of the Allies.

She had been involved, since the beginning of the war, which had now raged for four long years and it still looked unending – with the Japanese achieving such success in the Pacific. However, it was when her two sons – the pride and joy of her whole being – were both killed in action, one in Africa, one in Borneo, that in her grief, she had begun her 'White Feather' campaign.

It had come about at a gathering organized by the Red Cross. Eileen had stayed for afternoon tea when the meeting was over. Several of the committee started talking about the Australian men who were sneaking out of military service on trumped-up medical grounds, or other phoney reasons.

To Eileen's surprise she discovered that there were a large number of these shirkers and quite a number of shady doctors who were willing – for a fee – to falsify certificates. She became indignant and wanted to know what was being done to enforce conscription; indeed, became so vehement, that she became embarrassing to her fellow-workers.

Especially was this so, when she started writing letters to the Press, demanding that *all* doctors awarding military-exemption medical certificates be investigated.

With both her sons killed in action, Eileen's fury against those who, through trickery and fear, escaped the draft increased to an extent that she determined to shame all those she found in civilian clothes, by joining the groups of women who handed out the White Feather of cowardice.

As she left the tram, Eileen began to hurry to meet her daughter, Janice, at the little tea shop at the back of the Sydney Town Hall. She had noticed the time and discovered she was running late for the appointment. She decided to take the short cut through the narrow alley – it was quicker that way. She turned sharply left and entered the alley.

There was no sound as Lucky came up behind her. A hand came across her mouth from behind; she was dragged into the recessed doorway of an empty shop. Eileen struggled violently, but the man holding her was extremely strong. His right hand came round to her neck; his fingers pressed against her right carotid artery.

She began to choke, then as the pressure increased, started to lose consciousness. Removing his right hand from her neck, Lucky used his thin, very sharp, stiletto on both sides of the woman's face, drawing swift lines down her cheeks. There was stinging pain as the blood gushed freely.

With all her failing strength, Eileen fought madly, using her elbows and thrusting them into the man's stomach. She heard a grunt and for a moment, he swung her round, so that she was looking into the window at the *face* of her attacker reflected in the glass. Lucky looked up, saw himself and quickly struck the woman a sharp blow to the side of the head. Eileen knew no more.

Her struggles over, she lay in a tangled heap on the cement floor of the doorway.

Lucky quickly grabbed a handful of the feathers from Eileen's hat, and thrust them up her nose and into her mouth and ears. He inspected his clothes thoroughly to see he had no blood on him, wiped his knife across the woman's skirt and, checking that there was no one coming, walked quietly back to the tram stop.

He took out a cigarette, waiting calmly for the next tram, to get to the gym. Gone was the nervous tension that had troubled him earlier; he now felt relaxed and at ease ... he began to whistle softly.

Eileen's body was found an hour later. A young, female office worker found her and ran screaming for the police. The ambulance workers were surprised to discover the woman was still alive, but her face was shockingly mutilated. They were particularly horrified at what had been done with the feathers.

15

Sister Mary Luke stumbled as she passed Sister Josepha's office and clung, momentarily, to the door for support. The finance Sister jumped up and rushed to the terminally ill nun.

"Sister, what is it? Are you in great pain? Come, sit with me for a moment, or do you want me to get Mother?"

Sister Luke smiled, holding tightly onto the older woman's arm. "No, please Sister, don't tell Mother. She's at her wits end trying to cope with everything, then having me on top of it …"

"That's nonsense, Sister, and you know it. The whole house counts it a privilege to have you with us and Mother would drop everything in a moment if she thought she could help you." Sister Josepha went to take the very ill nun to a chair, but to her surprise, she resisted.

"Sister, could I ask a big favour of you?" she asked.

"It's done, if it's possible for me to do it," Josepha replied. "What would you like me to do?"

"Would you help me down the stairs, please? The sun is not so blazing hot today and I would just like to sit in the sun for a little while, where the nursery children are playing. Is that asking too much?"

"Consider it done. Let's take the stairs slowly and lean on me. I'm not much good in coping with people, but being a nurse, I'm pretty strong – tough actually – so you needn't worry about being too much for me."

Josepha put her arm around the fragile, wasted form of Luke and half-carried, half lifted, her down the stairs to the playground area. She called quickly to the nun playing with a group of noisy very small children.

Sister Francesca, taking in the situation at a glance, rushed for an old cane chair and had set it down in a partially shaded spot in the sun, by the time the two nuns reached it.

Francesca helped Josepha settle Luke in the chair then withdrew. Josepha sat on a stool beside the cane chair. She realised what suffering the stairs had cost the sick woman, so stayed quiet until the breathing was restored to something close to normal.

Sister Luke was looking at the children. "You know, Sister," she whispered, "I thought that's where God might let me work, when I became a nun – you know, with the tiny ones. They are the most precious ones, aren't they?"

"Yes, precious – the work of God's hands," Josepha replied.

Sister Luke's voice was so soft Josepha had to lean closer to hear her. The sick woman turned to look gratefully at her companion.

"You know, Sister, we sing those words, 'Magnalia Dei' and read them in Scripture so frequently, yet, *there* they are, in front of us: *the wonderful works of God*," the nun paused, altering her position slightly to help her breathing, then continued.

"But not just those innocent ones, but you, me, all the Sisters, the girls, big and small, the sun – beautiful in the blue sky – the birds; all that happens to each one of us – everything is included in …" She paused, and tried to take a big breath to continue talking, but was in difficulties. Josepha finished the sentence, "in Magnalia Dei – all are shining out as the wonderful works of God. Indeed, that's so very true, Sister; that little Latin phrase sums it up so perfectly.

"Every one of us is part of God's wonderful works and we *have* to believe that we are all involved in His whole plan, each one of us," Josepha's voice darkened and trembled, "no matter what happens, or what evil threatens us."

Sister Luke smiled her gratitude. Josepha turned her head away and spoke sadly. "But it's so easy to lose that awareness of innocence, isn't it, Sister? Those baby ones laughing there, could be ruined by evil parents, evil siblings, evil situations in which they find themselves – without any fault of their own."

"You speak strongly, Sister Josepha. Are you sure you're all right? … Are you troubled about anything? … Is anything wrong?" Luke asked painfully, struggling with each phrase.

"Yes, my dear child … *everything* is wrong and I don't know how to fix it – or even if I *can* ever undo the wrong," Josepha answered sorrowfully, her eyes filling with tears.

"Sister," urged Sister Luke, putting her thin hand on Josepha's arm. "Speak to Mother; you can tell her anything. She understands everything – and she will never, ever, condemn you, or cast you off, no matter what you might have done – or *think* you have done – however big or little."

Sister Luke began to speak again when they were rudely interrupted by the strident, insensitive voice of Sister Mary Margaret, Josepha's assistant, a tall nun with unsmiling eyes, and a sharp pointed nose. Her thin lips were pursed, disapprovingly.

"So that's where you are Sister Josepha! I've searched high and low for you. Have you forgotten we have a stack of work to do this morning? We have no time to be sitting around in the sun. I'm sure Sister Luke can look after herself; she doesn't need a nursemaid."

"Lower your voice, Sister Margaret," Josepha ordered sharply. "Take yourself back to my office and wait for me there. I shall stay here with Sister Luke a little longer."

"Well, I think a short brisk walk around the playground would do Sister Luke better than just sitting there, sunning herself. We can all imagine ourselves ill if we want to …"

Josepha's voice rose: "Cease talking immediately, Sister, or I shall report you to Mother. Leave us instantly." Sister Margaret was immediately incensed.

"Well, I like that. You can't even offer a word of advice to anyone in this place without having your head bitten off." Sister Margaret sniffed loudly in her indignation and flounced off – a mass of swirling, black-clothed umbrage.

Josepha turned to apologize to Luke, but was met with those enormous sunken eyes looking at her, with amusement and pity. She murmured something. Josepha moved her face closer to hear. Luke repeated the words: "Magnalia Dei, *even* Sister Margaret," and chuckled softly, then gasped, clutching at her side. "Sister, I'm sorry I'll have to go back, please help me ... I'm sorry."

Josepha nodded her understanding and bending, lifted up the frail body in her arms and carried it up the stairs and back to the infirmary. Gently putting Sister Luke down on the bed, Sister Josepha knelt beside the bed and humbly asked the young nun to bless her. "Benedicite," she murmured brokenly. Sister Luke smiled, as she said: "Deus."

Sister Josepha stayed where she was on the floor kneeling by the bed, until Luke had drifted into a light sleep.

16

Thursday

Lucky Falconi had a busy day Thursday. Before nine o'clock he drove the Falcon's large black car to the Girls' Reform Home at Tempe. Two girls were being released, and the Falcon had ordered them to be taken to Sarah's establishment.

The girls were waiting outside the gates when Lucky arrived. They were standing with a nun who was talking seriously with them. Lucky, wearing his chauffeur outfit, brought the car to a standstill, leapt from the driving seat, lifting his cap respectfully to the nun, who looked at him with shrewd eyes.

"Are you sure this is the man you were expecting, girls?" she asked doubtfully. Both Joan and Helen immediately said that it was. Helen added: "He works for my uncle; he's going to find us work to do, Sister. Don't worry about us; we'll be all right now. God bless you Sister."

The nun kissed each of the girls and as they drove off, stood waving until the car was out of sight uttering a short prayer that they might, just might, be all right.

She had been at the Reform Home for twelve years; no longer did she have any illusions about the girls who passed through their hands. "And if that load of lies, about the uncle, was the truth, then I'm the Archangel Gabriel! Oh, well, we can only do what we can."

She sighed and went back inside the gate, locking the steel doors securely behind her.

Out of sight of the Institution, Lucky leant over to the back seat and threw two packets of cigarettes to the girls. "Matches are in the side pockets of the car. Light up, I know you're dying for one, aren't you?"

"You're so sharp it's a wonder you don't cut yourself," Joan remarked as she lit the cigarette. "I hope this new place is better protected than the last place. I thought you paid the police enough to keep us safe there."

"We certainly do, but there was a new bloke on the beat who hadn't got the message; it's all fixed up now – he's been moved. You'll be safe with no need to worry."

"We'd better be," Helen remarked, "I have no intention of going back to that place. Being polite all the time to those nuns, was enough to make me want to throw up. And, as for the laundry work …"

"It's fair ruined my hands, it has," Joan moaned. "It'll take months to get them back to normal. Just look at the nails!"

"You'll be right with Sarah, girls," Lucky assured the girls, grinning. "She'll look after you. Now sit back and enjoy the ride."

17

Sarah Bellows was waiting in the vestibule of her establishment for the delivery of the two new girls. Sarah did not look like the common perception of a 'madam'. She was tall, beautifully groomed, stylishly but soberly dressed, in good, not flashy, clothes.

Her favourite colour was black, and with her still naturally golden hair parted in the middle in a Madonna style, with a large bun at the back, looked the very stereotype of the upper-middle-class, cultured, business woman of impeccable background. She was thirty eight years old.

Sarah felt she owed the Falcon, her boss, a debt of gratitude. It was he who had rescued her from abject poverty and a life on the streets, nineteen years ago, when he had taken into his care the young, frightened, newly pregnant girl he had found in the alleyway near his house.

She had been penniless and ill. She thought she would die alone and abandoned.

The man she had foolishly trusted, in her youthful ignorance, had cleared out after the second week she was with him. He left her, not only with child, but also with the burden of the rent he owed, which, when she had paid it, left her exactly nine shillings and sixpence halfpenny.

The Falcon was an astute opportunist. When he found Sarah, he could see – even in her distressed condition – that she had an innate dignity that indicated a good background. She was beautiful and elegant, even in distress. The Falcon noted her educated, cultured speech and thought there were possibilities there that could be exploited if he handled the situation carefully.

He would take the woman into his own house; order his daughter-in-law to look after her and, when the baby was born, he would arrange for it to be left at an Orphanage.

To safeguard his own interests, he would then tell Sarah that her baby had died. This would make her concentrate on the job he planned for her to do; she wouldn't be bothering her head then about a bastard kid.

He had also suggested that it would be better if Sarah changed her surname, which Sarah, believing that the Falcon had rescued her from the gutter, thought it was the least she could do, when this benefactor had asked for nothing in return.

It had all gone according to plan. Six weeks after the girl baby was born, the Falcon had informed Sarah, with touching sympathy, her child had died; it had not been strong enough to recover from the difficult birth. She was desolated; the Falcon visited her daily – the very picture of a saddened friend who shared her suffering.

It was only when Sarah had recovered from the shock of her child's death, the Falcon had then demanded re-payment. It was he who then taught her how to run the brothel business, then placed her with a trusted madam where Sarah served her apprenticeship.

She showed a flair for business management and, seeing this, the Falcon set her up in a place of her own and let her choose the girls she deemed right. He had long wanted a very respectable establishment which would attract the most discerning customers – the very top people – the politicians, the lawyers; the professional classes – who were prepared to pay handsomely for their pleasures, with the discretion required, for public figures.

The Falcon considered that, with Sarah, he had found the perfect 'hostess' to manage the establishment. He had also decided on the name. It was to be called, 'The Crosslands Gentlemen's Club'.

As the Club was to be select, many men would have to be turned away. Sarah would need protectors – muscle men – for this; the Falcon supplied them. Faithfully following the Falcon's directions, Sarah charged very large fees and therefore the girls had to be well trained, groomed and they needed to know how to speak courteously to the customers.

Sarah saw to this training personally. She gave the girls lessons in speech and manners, demanding a very high standard. Foul language, or vulgar speech, was punished with instant dismissal. The girls also needed to be regularly examined by doctors. There could never be a murmur of disease attached to her establishment. She had fulfilled every request that the Falcon had made of her, believing that he had acted through kindness in rescuing her, all those years ago. She was simply repaying her debt.

Sarah had done well. The Crosslands Gentlemen's Club was now well known in the right quarters, patronized by the right kind of men; it was very, very discreet. Sarah had a good amount now in the bank in her own name; the only regret that occasioned her sadness, as she was approaching forty, was for the baby girl who had died after she had been left at an Orphanage.

She often reflected sadly, if the child had lived, she could now have taken her from the Orphanage; she had plenty of money; she could have given the child a wonderful life, a life that she once had known herself, before she had foolishly ruined it.

She often sighed, but regrets were pointless – what else could she have done? At least I have a decent place to live, she thought; it's more than I thought I would ever have, after what I did.

At that moment the door opened and Lucky brought in the two new girls. Sarah looked at the new girls with distaste. Without a word of greeting, she led the way into her office. She then turned her eyes on the two young women. When she spoke her voice was ice-cold and authoritative.

"Get rid of those cigarettes immediately – they ruin your voice and make your mouth smell. Stand apart so I can see you." The girls did so, hastily stubbing out their cigarettes. "You," Sarah hastily glanced at the list in her hand, "Joan, undo that ridiculous tawdry thing in your hair – it is cheap and nasty – you look like a vulgar Christmas ornament. You are wearing too much lipstick – you will spend two hours this morning with Clarice learning how to use restrained make-up."

Sarah turned to the other girl, Helen. "You, Miss, have dyed your hair – how on earth did you get hold of dye in there? Never mind, it is coming out. You will see Hortense – the French hairdresser from Newtown; she's here today – to have the red dye removed and a soft honey shade used instead – or, perhaps a light brown; I'll leave that to Hortense.

"Right, the outfits you are wearing are frightful and useless – you look like tarts. When you take those clothes off, throw them into the furnace. This is a *Gentlemen's* Club. You will be wearing only decent, good quality clothes in this place, so you'd better get used to them. They are waiting in your room. When you have soaked in a perfumed bath, had your hair fixed, and your make-up altered, dress in the new clothes in your room and then come to me in my office. We will begin voice lessons this afternoon."

The girls pulled faces, then quickly smoothed out their expressions and nodded, as Sarah caught them. They were about to leave the madam when she made a decision.

"Give me the cigarettes now. No, *two* packets and the matches; you won't need them again. You haven't smoked while you've been inside – you will no longer smoke here. Go away and make yourself respectable – you are no use to us, until you are."

Sarah turned to Lucky and spoke coldly. "Lucky, the Falcon asked me to give you a package; it's a uniform of some sort. I'm sorry if it's not the right sort, but it was the only one I had in the wardrobe room so it'll have to do." She reached behind her desk, gave the parcel to Lucky, bade him 'Good Morning' frostily, and turned back into her office.

She had an intense dislike for the Falcon's grandson and felt no necessity to pretend otherwise. She was forced to work with him, but he knew well not to take any liberties with her; in private he called her the 'ice maiden'!

18

When Pamela Scott had finished her early morning chores at the Parker house, she and Mrs Thompson were having their morning tea.

They discussed the menu for the evening meal and Peggy Thompson informed Pamela which vegetables she would need to have ready. They sat in companionable harmony. Peggy liked the shy, courteous girl; she thought she was beautiful.

After last night, when Pamela had accidentally stumbled across the cook's personal tragedy – her drug-soaked daughter, Maureen – their relationship had changed; they were actually on the way to becoming real friends. Pamela hesitated, wondering if it were the right thing to do or not, then decided to tell the cook about the man she had met.

Immediately, Peggy was on the alert. She realised that this youngster, straight from an Orphanage, would be easy prey for any vicious and devious man on the make.

Peggy was also a realist. She knew that Pamela eventually *had* to meet a young man, somehow or other. It was always a bit of a lottery – you could so easily be fooled by appearances, but she could only hope that it would be a *decent* man.

She thought she'd try to warn Pamela about men – without sounding too much like a dragon.

"He sounds a very nice young man, dear. Does he work do you

know? You said he wasn't in a uniform. It's strange isn't it, today, to see a man who's not in one."

"Yes, I did ask him what he did, but I think it's something in the Government – I think he said something about the Defence Force Department – or, something like that."

"Well, of course, not everyone's in uniform. There are all the men who are in what they call, 'reserved occupations,' so he could easily be in something like that."

Peggy filled up the cups again. "I'd like to meet him, Pamela. Feel absolutely free to bring him home here. He could come to the kitchen on one of your days off, and we could have tea together. It'd be like inviting him to your own home."

Pamela's eyes lit up. "That'd be lovely, Mrs Thompson. I'd like you to meet Lucky."

"It's a funny nickname, isn't it love? What is his surname, do you know?"

"Yes," Pamela answered slowly. "A strange name, but I think I've got it right: Falconi, or something like that. I know it sounded like an Italian name."

"That's strange. He must be important, or have an important job, then. Most of the poor Italians are interned because of the war."

Peggy stood up. "Well, we'd better get going, love, there's still a lot to do. When you finish up-stairs, you could help me sort the laundry; we'll handle the ironing between us." As Pamela left the kitchen, Peggy's brow was wrinkled in thought. 'Falconi,' I've heard that name before, somewhere. I wonder why the name troubles me. Oh, well, on with the work.

Peggy had just turned back to the stove when she felt someone behind her who put his hand over her eyes and laughing, demanded: "And who's the best, good-looking, dashing, brilliant and most valiant, young barrister you've ever met?"

Peggy swung round, her face alight. "Well, it's definitely not John Parker I can tell you that!" she cried. "No, don't you dare swing me round, you young whipper-snapper. Just because you're six feet two, don't think I can't give you a good slap – as I once used to do."

The young barrister laughed and sat at the kitchen table. "Now, how are you my Second Ma? I'm only home for a couple of hours; we had a hell of a case this morning, but it's been held over – I think the Judge was drunk …"

"Sssh! John, don't say such things! People will believe them." Peggy sat down again opposite the young man and hastily checked to see if the tea was still hot. "I'll make you some fresh tea and I've just finished some scones that turned out pretty special if I do say so myself. Would you like to try some?"

'Would I ever? I've eaten nothing this morning. Was up studying this wretched brief most of the night; then to have the case held-over – all that good sleep I could've had – to say nothing of a good breakfast."

As Peggy hastened to get things ready for her favourite son of the house, she studied him carefully. John was a strong young man, nearly twenty-eight years of age, with short severely controlled brown hair, strong features, not strictly handsome, but good looking in a virile manner, with good hands and carefully manicured nails.

He was exquisitely dressed in a morning suit for court and hadn't changed before dashing home to see his parents. Court would resume in a couple of hours.

"Tell me, Second Ma, who was that pretty young woman who was leaving the corridor as I came charging in? I was bowled over; she's something special, isn't she?"

Peggy looked at the barrister seriously. "It's the new maid, John, from the Orphanage. She's a beautiful, innocent young girl; I think she's the best girl we've ever had. She's not only a splendid worker, but she's intelligent, compassionate and altogether lovely."

"What's her name?"

"It's Pamela, Pamela Scott. Mother Benedicta specially recommended her, your mother told me."

"Wow! That's high praise both from you and from the Lady Benedicta –I've met her, you know, the great lady, at some 'Charity Do' or other. This Pamela must be extra special." Peggy had a sudden thought.

"John, you're all involved with criminals and such people, aren't you?" John raised his eyebrows and pulled a comical face. Peggy hastened to correct her poor choice of words.

"No, that's badly put. I mean, you know a great number of the bad people – the crooks, I mean – who come up before you."

"You're right there. I know all the gangsters by now – one of the perks of the job," he laughed, then noticed the troubled look on Peggy's face. "Why, Second Ma, what's the problem?"

"Young Pamela told me that she's met a very nice young man whose name was Falconi … "

To her alarm, John shouted: "Good God! It's not the Falcon is it?"

"I don't understand …"

"No, forget that. Tell me, quickly, do you happen to know the first name?"

"I think she said it was a nickname – something like Lucky."

"No, for a moment, I was fearful that you were going to say Paolo Falconi – one of the three biggest gangsters in the Cross. Could be a relation, I suppose, but then again, it's probably a name like Jones – hordes of them. No, can't say I know of any Lucky Falconi."

"That's a relief, anyway," Peggy answered. "Now cover up those pretty trousers of yours with a couple of clean tea towels and try my scones. I've got some new strawberry jam, and …"

19

After driving the big black car back to the Falcon's house, Lucky Falconi quickly changed his clothes to a dark blue, unobtrusive suit, then with a briefcase under his arm, ran for the tram which took him to Central Railway Station; from there he caught a train to The Junction. He had decided to study the layout of the 'hit' now, while he had the time to do so.

Arriving at The Junction, he walked smartly through the shopping area and, just as he expected, came to the huge complex that was St Mary's Orphanage and Girls' Home. He had been told that it was large, but he didn't expect it to be *so* large – it was a huge complex.

The institution was surrounded by a high brick wall. Lucky could see the roofs of a number of two-storey buildings within the enclosure, while a very tall bell tower could be seen high above the Chapel. There was a gatehouse with a sign indicating where visitors were to come, while a little further down the street, there was another door that opened onto the street itself. That has to be the Chapel, he reasoned.

Lucky walked briskly to the door of the Chapel and, stepping inside, went up three steps and found himself in a small area just as his grandfather had described it.

In case anyone was looking – although the place looked empty – Lucky dipped his fingers in the Holy Water font and blessed himself, kissing his fingers afterwards, in the Italian manner. He then knelt with his head down in the very last row of the pews, just in front of a large statue of St Joseph.

His head was bent but his eyes darted everywhere. Yes, this little area would only hold about ten or twelve people at the most. He knew the Catholic custom of people popping in to a Church to make a 'visit', so understood why the door stood open all day.

Someone suddenly coughed slightly; Lucky's nerves jerked, while he held his breath.

He risked a quick side glance to his left and saw a very old man huddled in the corner of the pew with a rosary in his hand, his eyes tight shut and his lips moving silently. Lucky breathed again.

He then looked at the grill in front of the pews. It was made of steel, painted black and formed to make openings each about one square foot in area. It stretched from one wall of the Chapel to the other. In the middle of the grill there was a Communion hatch, waist high, which, obviously, could be opened from within, when needed.

Through the grill, Lucky saw that he would have no difficulty in seeing the nuns. There were two rows of choir stalls on each side of the Chapel; the row closest to the wall raised three feet higher than the one in front. He was interested to see directly in front of him, in line with the altar, a throne-like wooden chair with its own kneeler – separate from the other stalls.

That must be for the Big Boss Lady, he thought – the dame in charge of all this. Lucky looked past the big chair to the altar. The Sanctuary was large and the altar was of white marble, the pulpit marble as well. Where do they put the kids, he wondered? Then he noticed a side Chapel that stretched out of sight to the right of the altar.

He thought the side Chapel was obviously for the girls, but this place is the one he wanted.

At that moment Lucky had another shock. A large bell began to ring the Angelus and as it continued ringing, nuns began entering through a door up near the altar. First came a dumpty elderly nun who, after genuflecting to the altar, stumped briskly down the Chapel aisle and climbed the steps to her chair that Lucky had noticed.

So, she's the boss; just as he thought. The other nuns entered the Church, genuflected to the altar. Then turned and bowed to the Superior, who remained standing at her special place.

Lucky grinned. This was going to be easier than shooting ducks at the local fair – he couldn't fail to hit one; they would be coming straight towards him as they took their places.

No one took any notice of him and no one entered the public section of the Chapel while he was there. As the chant began, Lucky rose, genuflected slowly, carefully dipped his fingers in the font and blessed himself again – it always paid to be cautious.

He then left the building.

Outside, Lucky wanted to whistle. This was going to be a piece of cake, he chuckled to himself. Nonno will be so proud of him. Now that he had studied the layout of the Chapel, Lucky thought he'd better check out the rest of the street while he was there. He found, next to the Orphanage, the parish Church and Presbytery.

A very old priest was seeing someone off at the gate, so Lucky said immediately, 'Good morning, Father,' as he passed and moved on quickly. The priest answered, but the woman to whom he was talking, paused a moment, stared at the man's back, then grabbed violently at the arm of the priest, her face drained of colour and her lips beginning to tremble as she agitatedly tried to speak.

Lucky caught the train back to Central, and then, fifteen minutes later, was back home, sitting at his desk planning what he would do with Pamela the next day – Friday. He had it all worked out; it just needed some fine tuning to get it right.

He had decided to begin the day by bringing the girl to his home.

He knew it would be a risk Pamela meeting his mother, but it could work out well. It'd better, he muttered, or else the old woman would feel his open hand across her face.

She knows better than to refuse to cooperate with me, when I'm involved in the Falcon's business.

20

When Mrs Eileen Hodges' face had been stitched in the casualty section of the city hospital, she had been given a blood transfusion. Eileen then claimed she was ready to go home. She declared that, apart from the shock, she was perfectly well and demanded she be released.

Her daughter Janice and son-in-law, Judge Maurice Bernstein, urged her to remain in hospital, at least until she had recovered sufficiently from the shock, but Eileen was adamant; she was going home.

Her face was covered with sticking plaster over the stitches; the clear patches of skin of her face, a blue/black smudge of bruising, while a bandage was tightly bound around her head with a pad over the spot where she had been struck.

Finding it useless trying to persuade her otherwise, the Judge and his wife, exasperated with the obstinate woman, waited until Eileen signed herself out of the hospital. Despite her protestations of complete recovery, the elderly woman was glad to hold on to her daughter's arm as she was helped to the Judge's car to be driven home.

The Judge sat in the front seat with his driver, while Janice sat with her mother in the back. They talked little on the journey; the daughter tight with anger at the foolishness of her mother in doing what she had been doing.

She had warned Eileen so many times that one day she would

give the white feather to the wrong kind of person; now her warnings had been fulfilled with a vengeance. Janice had determined on a plan.

"When we get home, Mother, I'm putting you straight to bed and there you will stay until at least Sunday. Try to remember, it was only yesterday that you went through that frightful ordeal." Janice's voice trembled. "You could easily have been killed; it's a miracle you weren't. When you're completely rested, Maurice and I want to have a little talk with you, but we won't go into that now. We'll just get you home first."

"No, we won't," Eileen answered tartly. "First, we'll call at the Presbytery at The Junction. I want to see Father O'Shea, just for a moment."

She forestalled the next protest. "I promise you. I'll only stay a moment. I want to see him alone, then you can have your way; I'll stay in the damn bed for a couple of days, but if you think I'm staying longer than that, you can think again."

Janice sighed, and gave new directions to the driver, while in the front seat, the Judge also sighed and rolled his eyes.

21

Father O'Shea had listened to Mrs Hodges patiently, and wisely didn't say what he really thought of her foolish behaviour. He realised that she was still in a state of shock and wisely nodded, listened, then led the elderly woman slowly to the front gate of the Presbytery. The Judge and his wife were waiting patiently in the car.

They stood for a couple of minutes outside the gate as the big bell was ringing the Angelus from St Mary's. The priest promised he would look in on Eileen in a couple of days if she were not at Mass on Sunday and assured her he would pray for her.

A young man hurried past them on the pavement and said, "Good Morning, Father." The Priest returned the greeting and was about to take Eileen to the car, when he was startled to see she had turned white with shock. Clutching at his arm in terror, she whispered: "That's the man! I swear before God, that *is* the man!" Her eyes rolled upward in her head and she fainted.

The priest was just in time to catch her before she hit the pavement. The judge, his wife and the driver leapt from the car and rushed to the elderly priest's assistance. The young man had disappeared from sight.

22

Friday

On Friday morning the late summer sun rose sparkling in a cloudless blue sky. It was warm but not with the stifling heat of the previous weeks. There was a definite feeling in the air that autumn was not too far away.

Lucky rose from bed, did the push-ups he did each morning, then, instead of just ringing, to inform his mother that he was ready for breakfast, he decided to go upstairs and have the meal with her.

Angelina was disturbed when her son appeared at the kitchen door. He then made it clear he was staying with her this morning. She hastened to give him everything he asked for, keeping silent, wondering what he was after – this was too unusual for it to be normal.

When she had placed food before her son, he looked up at her and spoke in a cold, menacing, voice: "Listen, carefully, old woman. I'm bringing a young girl here today to meet you. The Falcon wants it, so be on your best behaviour. She's very young, straight out of an Orphanage and, remember this, she's very religious.

"I want you to be very nice to her, speak nicely about me; tell her how I look after you, provide you with money, help you to get to Church whenever you want. Understand?"

Angelina's fingers were pleating the apron she wore with nervous energy. "What do you want with the girl? Why is she coming here?

What are you going to do with her? Where are you taking her?"

"What's the meaning of these questions? What's it got to do with you? Just do as you've been told. If you don't, I'll tell Nonno. You know what happened to Papa; I'd be sorry to hear you went the same way ... you're a good cook."

Lucky laughed loudly, he thought that was pretty funny and helped himself to another slice of toast. His mother moaned with anguish, holding the apron up to her eyes. So this is the poor little lamb they are going to destroy, is it – and they expect her to take part in her ruin?

Angelina's mind started to race. Could I warn her? How? The poor girl could be besotted with Lucky – he's all false charm, but so deadly dangerous! Worse than dangerous, he'll take her to the Falcon; that's the end of her!

Angelina summonsed up her courage and standing up straight with her hands clenched by her sides, spoke with intensity to her son.

"God will destroy you, and *him* – *him* upstairs, if you harm this girl. I am telling you Francis, you will be destroyed utterly."

Angelina came forward, and touched her son timidly. "It isn't too late, Francis, you could start again. You could break with the Falcon, get away; begin all over again. Francis. You know that anyone who curses God, or harms the little ones – the innocent ones – will, in turn, be cursed by God and ..."

Lucky got up, slowly and deliberately, from the table, went over to the large crucifix hanging on the wall, then carefully spat at the figure. Angelina screamed, and then covering her face in her apron, began to rock to and fro.

Lucky looked at his mother, indifferently and, as he was leaving, said over his shoulder: "She's be here in about an hour, have morning tea ready for her; be careful old woman, one wrong step and you'll end up like Papa."

He began to whistle, as he casually left the room, now feeling excited as he always was when he had proven his power over anybody; strangely excited also, at the prospect of seeing Pamela again and bringing her home.

Lucky left the house and thought briefly about the old woman, then dismissed her. She'll do what she's told; she had no option, had she? He laughed. He walked quicker in an unusual hurry to see Pamela again, feeling happy and different, for some reason. I'm really actually looking forward to this, he realised, slightly bewildered.

Just as quickly this mood changed – as it did frequently these days – but, perhaps … I won't!

His steps slowed and his euphoric feeling started to dissipate. He remembered what his mission was to be today; it wasn't just a 'day-out' – it was work; he had a job to do.

As his steps slowed, his mood became dark; he had an unusual sensation of oppression. For some strange reason, he was suddenly reluctant to bring Pamela to his house; to introduce her to his mother; to begin the process of turning her into a tart...

Why ever not? She's the type the Falcon wants. I've done this so many times before; what's different now? Lucky stopped completely and leant against a fence … thinking …

He had fantasized about Pamela ever since he had found her on the park bench. In his mind, he saw her clearly: the unfashionable clothes, the modest deportment, the obvious child-like trust; those beautiful clear, innocent eyes so full of trust.

He was mystified; Pamela was *different* from the others! *Why* was she different, he pondered? He answered himself hesitatingly: because she was *totally* innocent – *like a child*! That's why!

Never ever could he recall ever meeting a truly innocent young woman before – this disturbed him; the innocent girl was dangerous, in some way – dangerous to *him*.

In an unusual way this girl had stirred him, frightened him; that had never happened before; he felt suddenly out of his depth – in uncertain territory; there was a vague, fleeting glimpse of the possibility of another sort of life.

Why, he wondered, did it seem *dangerous* to touch her; why was that? She was just another girl. *Why* was *he* concerned with what happens to her? He hadn't been with all the others. Why this one?

He half-jeered at himself as he wondered if this was what the Movies meant when they drivelled on and on about 'love'?

Could he possibly be *in love with the girl*? He flushed with shame and looked around quickly, as if the thought itself could be overheard. What would the Falcon say if he heard him say *that* aloud! Or, even *noticed* his attitude in regard to this girl?

Whatever the cause of this strange infatuation, for the first time in his life, Lucky indulged in fancies about the two of them …could they have had a life together? Was it *possible* for men like him to have … what they call … a 'normal' life?

Lucky was unsure of himself suddenly; the path was no longer clear-cut; it was a maze and he was in the centre trying to find his way out; in very serious danger of becoming totally lost.

He had never felt this way about any of the numerous girls that had come his way in the course of his work for Nonno. This was unique!

He began to understand why this was so: he did not *know* any girls like Pamela: there was something *untouchable* about her.

Now, the vague – Movie-like – dream was going to be shattered; he was going to kill one of the women Pamela most probably loved at that damn Orphanage! If she ever found out about that, she would *hate* him; shudder with loathing if he came near her!

No, she could never love him, she could only fear and detest him.

And, then … he closed his eyes … to think of what's going to happen to her when I hand her over to the Falcon! All those revolting filthy old men! He closed his eyes and shuddered.

Lucky knew his role now was only to groom her, so she could be turned over to Sarah. Lucky was sure – once the Falcon had seen this girl – he would want her for the classy Crosslands Club. The

Falcon had told Lucky he had phoned Sarah earlier telling her he might be sending a new girl for her to assess this morning.

He sighed, feeling suddenly older and, for some reason, bitter and weary.

He started to walk again and thought suddenly of his mother. She was friends with normal people with ordinary jobs; wives with husbands and kids. Was it possible there could be a life for him outside the Falcon's tiny world – a bit like the world his mother lived in – not the looney, mad bits – but the good bits?

After all, what about the good, decent, women and men who wouldn't even know about the goings-on in Kings Cross? There *must* be a different world somewhere … where to be *decent* was 'normal'.

Or was he just being childish? Was the world of the Movies a possibility, or really just make-believe? In the Movies, everyone is nice, well dressed, clean, had kids that they seemed to love and spoke without all the adjectives he heard, and used, every day of his life.

Or was it all really just lies? Perhaps … perhaps… as his grand-father had said so often, *his* kind of life was all that life *had* to offer?

There was nothing else! That's what Nonno had always said. How many times Nonno had said Lucky's mother was a moron, *because* she believed there *was* something else?

If that's true, he'd be a fool to throw any of it away. What would he have left if he gave up his life with Nonno? Nothing! He'd *be* nothing; he'd *have* nothing! What else could he do? What sort of life would that be?

No! It'd be stupid! And, *he* wasn't stupid! There were mugs galore; he was *not* going to be a mug.

No, a mug is a loser; he had no intention of being a loser.

Lucky cleared his throat and spat in the gutter...

He straightened up and shook his head; he had come to a decision.

Enough of this! He had a job to do; concentrate on that. Get this job done with Pamela, charm her today, hand her over to Sarah, and … … *forget her.*

There's plenty of other girls, just waiting; he'd be an idiot to give up what he had for a vague dream that probably … was all moonshine … all Hollywood fantasy anyway.

23

On Friday, for her day out, Pamela Scott wore her second best dress – she only had two good ones. She hurried, knowing that Lucky would be waiting for her. She bought a take-away cup of coffee and took it to the little park where they had first met. To her surprise Lucky was already there.

He jumped up as he saw her and she blushed with pleasure. Lucky held out his hand; Pamela shook his hand politely and then went to sit down. Lucky prevented her from doing so by keeping hold of her hand.

"Pamela, I thought today we'll make it a special day for your day off. Firstly I'd like you to meet my mother. I've told her you might be coming for morning tea. Will that be all right? We only live a short walk away." Lucky put on his diffident look; he gave the impression he was worried he had presumed too much. Pamela was touched.

"I'd love to meet your mother, Lucky." She carefully poured out her coffee onto the flower beds and put the container in the bin. "Please let me buy a little bunch of lavender to take to her. I love lavender and I saw some as I was buying the coffee."

"Flowers?" Lucky was bewildered; flowers for the old woman? He rapidly pulled himself together. "Why … that's … that's a lovely thought. Yes, let's go and buy the flowers. Mum will like that. She'll be surprised."

I bet she will, he thought, it'll be the first time she's ever received flowers – except the bunch from her husband's grave.

He was surprised to suddenly remember she had kept those flowers, until they had fallen to pieces, the petals littering the floor.

They bought the little bunch of lavender and walked the four blocks to the Falcon's house. Pamela was amazed at the obviously wealthy, huge, terrace house which looked spotlessly clean and meticulously maintained. "Oh, it's so lovely, Lucky," she breathed.

They went up the main entrance steps and Lucky rang the bell. Angelina answered the door apprehensively. Pamela was confronted by a tall woman with beautiful black eyes and eyebrows, her grey hair escaping from the black scarf tied under the chin. The woman seemed to be covered in black: head scarf, shawl and a long black dress. Her fingers were nervously smoothing her black shawl over the dress.

When Pamela was timidly invited inside, she immediately gave the lavender to the grey haired woman and feared for a moment that she had given offence. The Italian woman stared in amazement at the flowers, slowly smelled the beautiful perfume, and then, to Pamela's surprise, smiled, and took the startled girl into her arms, hugging her tightly.

Pamela, thinking the elderly, fearful woman was shy, and apparently did not know what to say, decided to take the initiative. She took the older woman's hand and led her to the religious pictures on the walls, chatting freely.

"Why, Mrs Falconi, I know these beautiful pictures! They're the same as we have back at the Girls' Home where I come from; they're wonderful. Do you know what?" she asked, holding the old woman's arm closely, "whenever I pray to Mary, I always call her Holy Mother." She laughed gently. "Oh, you have lovely things here, Mrs Falconi! Thank you for letting me see them. Oh! Look at this!" Pamela had just seen the very fine silver crucifix hanging on one wall. "It's beautiful!"

She heard a gasp from Lucky's mother, and turned to see her

holding both hands upwards, praying audibly; but she also noticed Lucky looking furious and embarrassed.

Pamela quickly tried to change the subject and moved away from Angelina, towards some photographs on a small table. She had noticed a little picture of a young woman in a small frame and thought this could be a safe subject.

"Oh, what a lovely girl! Is that your daughter?" she asked. The result of this innocent question was alarming. The Italian woman rushed forward with a terrified glance at her son.

"No, I have no daughter," Angelina grabbed the small photo and put it quickly into a drawer.

"But … the girl in the picture? She's a beautiful young woman. You must be very proud of her." The Italian woman began to cry. Pamela hurried to her side. "Oh, I'm so sorry. Is something wrong? Please forgive me. I'm always saying the wrong thing."

"No, no … not that! Dead, she's dead. My husband, my son, my daughter… all dead."

Pamela was confused. She took the woman gently by the hand. "But Lucky is your son; he's not dead." She was immediately contradicted by the woman. "Yes, dead," and began to weep uncontrollably. Pamela looked helplessly at Lucky, tears in her eyes.

"I'm so sorry; I have said the wrong thing. I think, Lucky, I'd better leave. I'm upsetting your mother in some way. I'm sorry I didn't mean to do so."

The young girl was surprised to see the anger on Lucky's face. He was scowling at his mother and spoke, through gritted teeth, roughly to her in Italian. The distraught woman cowed in the corner, her shawl now pulled up, covering her head.

Lucky clipped his tongue in disgust, and taking Pamela's hand, pulled her towards the front door.

"I'm sorry Pamela. I thought a little visit would delight her. She's a difficult woman." Lucky then tried to make the situation Pamela had witnessed a little more plausible.

He stammered: "She's never got over the death of her husband – I think it has affected her mind. This morning was a good morning for her; I thought it would be safe to bring you here. Let's go, we'll have morning tea at Sarah's place; she's waiting to meet you."

Pamela let herself be taken from the room. When she looked back to smile and wave goodbye to Mrs Falconi, her eyes opened in astonishment. The elderly woman was looking intently at her, her face anguished; she was shaking her head furiously from side to side, while pointing to her son's back. Pamela hurried from the house bewildered. The woman was warning her of something.

It couldn't be that she meant her own son, could it? No, it couldn't be that; it wouldn't make sense. Angelina's litany kept repeating itself in her head: My husband, my son, my daughter, all dead; my husband, my son, my daughter, *all dead*. Pamela shivered in apprehension; a strange awareness of evil seemed to have descended on her for the first time in her life.

In her fear, she held tightly onto Lucky's arm. She was confused and suddenly very afraid, but of what, or of whom, she did not know.

24

Sarah Bellows was waiting to receive her guests in her own small, comfortable sitting room of the Crosslands Gentlemen's Club.

Lucky had explained to Pamela that Sarah ran a very select Club for Gentlemen; a good number of girls worked for her. They held important positions and earned large salaries. Sarah was busy getting the tea things ready and had been advised by the Falcon that he wanted this girl, so she had used the good china. It was only when Lucky came into the room that Sarah saw the girl for the first time.

Sarah had been holding the good teapot; in her shock, she almost dropped it.

She stared at Pamela in astonishment, beginning to tremble; it was as if she were staring into a mirror. This wasn't possible …? Such things couldn't be …? Her mind screamed: *The child was dead; dead, dead, dead!* She had been *assured of that* by the Falcon; *THE BABY HAD DIED! … SHE WAS DEAD!*

Lucky was aware something was wrong. He attempted to normalise the situation:

"Sarah, this is Pamela Scott."

Sarah paid no attention to Lucky, but she heard the *name* 'Scott'. Faced with the young woman, her mind was in turmoil: she dared to ask herself – for the very first time – had it been the truth? Or… *did that man lie to her?*

My God! Had she been a gullible fool all these years? If what she thought could be true… then her whole life had been wasted!

Her mind raced. But, would the Falcon have lied? Yes, he *would*! She knew him well; if it suited his purposes he would tell any lie whatsoever; but, when she'd been helpless, she had believed him utterly!

But …be careful! It might just be one of those strange coincidences … But, her mind screamed, there was the *name, as well*! She tried to control her surging thoughts and desperately attempted to concentrate on the situation she was now in.

There was complete silence in the room. Lucky was beginning to show his irritation. He watched, in bewilderment, as Sarah stared at the girl.

What the hell was wrong with the stuck-up bitch? He knew she hated him, but no one left him standing there looking like a jerk.

He was just about to tell the woman what he thought of her, when Sarah's eyes went to him.

She quickly realised how dangerous this situation was. If there was any hope of saving this girl, she was ruining it by letting that man see how shocked she was.

Sarah's mind clicked in; it began to function and she realised what she was doing … *in front of Lucky* – she knew full well of what he was capable.

She must answer him quickly. Pulling herself together with an effort, Sarah's face, which had blanched with the shock, began to regain some colour. She made them sit down and started to make small talk as she poured the tea.

But, try as she might, Sarah felt her senses reeling each time she looked at Pamela and her voice failed. She closed her eyes tightly and tried to start again.

"And, you come from a Home, Lucky tells me, Pamela," Sarah swallowed and forced her voice to sound coldly impersonal.

"Yes, that's right Miss Bellows," Pamela answered. The girl

looked around her. "You have a very big place to manage here. Lucky has explained about this exclusive Club. It looks very grand and expensive to me, like those wonderful hotels you see at the Pictures."

"Yes, it is very beautiful," Sarah answered, mechanically. "Tell me, Pamela, how old are you. Please forgive me if that sounds rude, but you look so young."

"It's not rude at all, Miss Bellows. I am nearly eighteen. I have been in the Orphanage since I was born, but I've had a good education and the nuns were wonderful; I love them dearly, especially Mother Benedicta." Pamela smiled, "I call her my mother for that's what she's like to me. I've never known any other mother."

To Sarah, that innocent remark of Pamela's was utter anguish. She turned her head away, thinking I shall burst into tears, or else scream, in a minute. She pretended to cough politely to give her a moment's respite. She didn't know how she was going to manage to continue – with Lucky watching her all the time.

She struggled to keep the conversation going. "I'm very happy to hear that you have a happy memory of your upbringing, my dear child. I shall certainly send a special donation to the institution because of that. Which one was it?"

"It's St Mary's Orphanage and Girls' Home at The Junction, Miss Bellows, and whatever you send there, will be thankfully received. It was only as I grew older that I realised how desperately hard the nuns worked, just trying to keep the place going and to feed all of us.

"As soon as I get a raise, I'm going to send something each payday to Mother – it's the least I can do. They have done everything for me; they even found me a parlourmaid position with wonderful, kind and good people: the Parkers, in Lilac Street, do you know them?"

"I haven't had that pleasure I'm sorry, Pamela. Perhaps one day I might. So, you're happy there working as a maid?"

"Yes, I know it doesn't sound very smart or grand, but it's good work and I'm a good worker. The nuns taught me shorthand and typing and perhaps, one day, I might try to get an office job – the money would be more I know, but I think I'd miss Mrs Thompson, the cook, who has become a close friend to me – the Parker family who are so kind to me as well. I really feel at home there."

"Pamela, you have a pretty name. How did you get it? Do the Sisters give the babies a name when they have them baptized?"

"That's what's usually done. But, in my case, there was a name pinned to my clothes. Apparently my mother – my real mother, that is," Pamela smiled gently, "wanted the baby to be called that and so the nuns did. I'm glad for I have something of my mother at least."

Sarah stood up. "Please excuse me a moment, dear. I'll be back in a moment." She hurried into her inner office and leaned against the door screwing her eyes tightly closed. How on earth can I keep this going in front of *him?* She took deep breaths and then, forcing her face to reveal nothing, returned to the room. She turned to Lucky.

"You're very quiet, Lucky, for a change. How on earth did you find this beautiful young girl? *Tell* me," she added in a tone that indicated she was not at all pleased, and demanded an honest answer.

Lucky answered her, describing the chance meeting in the lunch hour. He was now anxious to leave; he had not expected this reaction from Sarah. They disliked each other, but had always been courteous and polite before. Now, Sarah looked as if she positively hated him and would delight in poisoning him.

He felt uneasy; anxious to get away, so, at the first opportunity, told of his plans to take Pamela for a ferry ride to Watson's Bay. They would have lunch there. Pamela had only been on a ferry once before.

Sarah said, frostily, that it all sounded very nice indeed and stood up.

When Pamela stood up to leave, to her surprise, Sarah leant towards her and kissed her lightly on the cheek, promising that she would be in touch with her shortly. She asked if the young girl would take her one day – on her day off – to see the place where she had been brought up.

Pamela was delighted that this grand and beautiful lady would be interested in an Orphanage and promised that she would go with her any time it could be arranged. They took their leave; Sarah speaking to Pamela only, ignoring Lucky completely.

As soon as the two young people had left, Sarah, with shaking hands, dialled the Falcon. When he answered she spoke fiercely with tightly suppressed rage:

"You *lied* to me. I trusted you and you lied to me! My child did *not* die. She is alive and working here in this area and that evil monster of a grandson of yours has her in his power."

The Falcon went to interrupt. "No, *you* listen to me, Falcon, I'm warning you, if any harm comes to Pamela Scott – Scott is *my real* name, remember – I'll blow the whistle on you and all of you. I'm not asking you, I'm telling you: order Lucky to drop her, to leave her alone. I won't take her in here and that's that and I'll move heaven and earth to prevent you, *and him*, from putting her in any other of your bloody hell holes."

She slammed down the receiver and sitting down burst into tears, her hands pressed to her mouth to soften the sounds of her anguish. Her only plan now must be to help the child escape the power of the Falcon and remove her from the evil creature, the grandson … but *how*, in the name of heaven, was she to do that?

25

Pamela was very quiet on the ferry. When Lucky asked her if she felt all right she promptly assured him she did, and that the ferry ride was wonderful.

When she raised her eyes and looked at the glorious Sydney Harbour she thought this was the most beautiful sight she had ever seen. She gazed in wonder at the large number of war ships in the harbour; there seemed to be dozens. She realised that all the Americans she had seen in the crowded streets of the Cross must have come from these ships.

Lucky, seeing her interest, began to point out the scenic highlights of the beautiful harbour, the names of the islands, the famous historic, convict-built, Pinchgut Fort, and the dazzling view of the Heads – where the ocean began. The summer sun was glistening on the waves and made her eyes dazzle.

However, in spite of the beauty before her, Pamela's thoughts were travelling back and forth over the extraordinary morning she had had: the strange, disturbing, behaviour of Lucky's mother, then the equally strange affinity, mixed with unease, she had felt with the Sarah lady.

Even with Sarah… lady that she obviously was, the behaviour had been …odd …puzzling. She hoped she would have the chance to see the beautiful woman again.

Her mind drifted to her companion standing at her side at

the rail. And Lucky? What did she really know of Lucky? Pamela was honest enough to answer her own question. Nothing, really… except what he had told her.

A vague suspicion began to disturb her thoughts. How come he could just take days off when it suited him – if his job was as important as he had implied? If it were that important, wouldn't it mean that he would rarely have time off, in time of war? The more she thought about it, the more mysterious it all was. Lucky *must* be working.

He certainly seemed wealthy enough: his clothes were very expensive; he must have an income from somewhere or other. Perhaps from the grandfather he had mentioned? Pamela began to feel uneasy. Mrs Thompson's guarded warning had not been lost on her – she *was* inexperienced, she knew that, but she was not dumb.

Oh well, she shrugged, it's all too much for me. I'll just try to enjoy this ferry trip; it might be the last one I'll get.

Arriving at Watson's Bay, she held her dress modestly in the wind blown up from the ocean, as she stood with Lucky at the famous 'suicide spot' called the 'Gap'. Lucky had no fear of heights and was standing on the very edge of the cliffs, looking down at the jagged rocks below.

He urged her, playfully, to come and stand beside him. She edged closer, but after one terrified look over the side of the cliff, retreated to the safety of the fence rail.

Lucky laughed, saying a good meal would make all the difference to her fears. There was a wonderful restaurant at Watson's Bay, but you could also buy excellent fish and chips to take away as well, so they decided to do this.

They sat in a shaded, outdoor area to eat their dinner, and were soon surrounded by dozens of sea-gulls who ate their scraps which made them both laugh. The tension eased between them and Pamela relaxed, beginning to feel ashamed of her doubts regarding her young man.

After the meal Pamela felt much happier and apologized to Lucky, for being such a miserable companion. He immediately assured her he understood; she had had a distressing morning; he apologized again for taking her to meet his mother.

He stressed he had really thought it was one of her good days; he'd been terribly wrong. He suggested they walk by the shore and he held Pamela's hand lightly.

Pamela felt her fears and suspicions quietly slip away. He must be a good man, she tried to reassure herself, he is gentle, loving and kind, but why is he also so ... *mysterious*? Perhaps it is his 'hush-hush' job that makes him like that? Or ... is it?

Pamela decided to give up her unprofitable speculations and tried to lose herself in the enchantment of the wonderful, natural, beauty of the harbour – the sunlight sparkling in the shimmering light of the sun as it danced upon the white capped waves.

She knew time was running out; she would soon have to return to the Parker's house. They were expecting visitors today for afternoon tea, and Pamela had promised that she would return early, to help Mrs Thompson serve the tea.

With Lucky at her side, Pamela walked slowly back to the ferry for the return trip.

It had been a pleasant and interesting day; however, Pamela was surprised to discover she felt strangely relieved that this precious 'day-out' was very nearly over.

26

Judge Maurice Bernstein was often irritated by his mother-in-law, Eileen Hodges, and proud of her at the same time. She has the courage of a lion, he thought – *and* the strength.

He felt himself tremble, as he remembered her vivid and detailed description of her assailant; he knew at once who it was – that monster, Falconi's grandson.

He had seen a photo of him on the Falcon's desk during that terrible visit he had made to the gangster. Now that Eileen had given the description to the police, it was only a matter of time before they matched the picture they had drawn up, to the actual criminal.

Then what, he asked himself? The judge closed his eyes in near panic.

What if the Falcon used his threat again of publishing the phoney photos to get Lucky off the hook? The judge's lips firmed into a thin line as he made a sudden decision. Come what may, he was not going to dance to the Falcon's tune ever again. I should never have even visited the man in his house – that alone compromises me.

In his agitation, he struck the table with his fist.

In my position, he thought miserably, one cannot afford to put a foot wrong – the press will crucify you; he must have been out of mind visiting that man! The old saying flashed through his mind: Curiosity killed the cat! Well, it had nearly killed him …and still could!

At that moment, Eileen came into the sitting room on Janice's arm.

"Maurice, we have a problem," Janice announced, "Mother insists on going to Vespers on Sunday afternoon at the Home. I've talked her out of trying to get to Mass Sunday morning, but it's only on condition that we take her to Vespers in the afternoon." Janice looked appealingly at her husband. "What do you think? Should she go, or not?"

Maurice's good humour was restored by the question; he smiled at his mother-in-law. "Eileen, what would it matter what I think? If you have decided that you're going to Vespers, then I know full well, you'll be going." They all laughed. Eileen looked with affection at her son in law.

"Maurie, you're a good man. I knew you'd understand. I can't just lie about pretending I'm an invalid. Apart from a general soreness in the face and a slight headache, I'm perfectly recovered."

"You'd never think so, looking at you," laughed the Judge. "You look as if you've been in the ring with a boxer." Eileen smiled and touched her son-in-law's arm gently. "Then you'll take me to Vespers, you and Janice?" she pleaded.

"Anything for a quiet life," agreed Maurice. "However, don't get any idea of converting me, Eileen. Let me remind you that, we Jews, have been saying and singing the psalms even longer than you Christians."

"That's true, Maurice, but I still have hopes – even of you." which made them all laugh again.

Eileen sighed. "I can't wait for Sunday but I suppose I must." She sat down in one of the big chairs. "Janice, give me that damn khaki jumper you were knitting; I'll finish it off for the Red Cross – it'll give me something to do."

The judge smiled indulgently. Well, she's a good woman, even if she's eccentric, so what's the big deal about going to Vespers on Sunday? It will please the elderly lady and Janice as well. I'm not likely to meet anyone I know there who's been up before me on the bench, or that anything's likely to happen. Perhaps a nice quiet, tranquil religious service, with gentle chanting, is just what the old lady needs after the trauma of the vicious assault.

The judge was a gentle, pleasant man in his home life and a very great scholar in his own field; he had many gifts. Unfortunately, for his own peace of mind, prophecy was not one of them.

27

"Mary, it was kind of you to invite us for afternoon tea," Monica Jeffrey said as she and her cousin entered the Parker's house. "This is my cousin, Anne Watson, who's been staying with me for the last couple of days."

Mrs Mary Parker smiled at her visitors and advanced on Annie with hand outstretched. "Mrs Watson, I can't tell you how delighted I am to meet you. I know all about you, from Monica here."

Annie Watson shook hands and smiled. 'Please call me Annie, Mrs Parker. I am getting spoilt here with Monica. Everyone is so polite and courteous to me – it's quite unnerving! In my little village, people are so used to me they think I'm a 'stand-in' for the village idiot!" Everyone laughed. Mary shook her head, smiling.

"Thank you Annie; please call me Mary. No, you can't get away with that. You see I have a spy in this house, who knows all about you and talks about you often."

"Oh, dear, that always frightens me!" Annie cried, trying to pin up her hair which was starting to come loose. "I told Monica to pretend that we're not related – people will think she's like me. But," she asked smiling. "Who is the spy in the house? Tell me so I can be on my guard and pretend to be normal."

"Why, my own son, John. He's a barrister too, just like your son-in-law, George McKenzie."

"Goodness gracious me! The world's really a tiny place isn't it?

Well, I certainly do know George, my own very dear son-in-law – have known him all his life; he was born in the house of his parents. He's a fine lad, and I'm sure that your boy is also."

Annie lowered her voice. "Mrs Parker, I know about your own tragedy. Words are useless aren't they? So I won't add any inane remarks. I, too, have a son who is ill, and we've nearly lost him a number of times, so I know what it is like."

Annie's voice brightened. "But tell me about your son, the barrister. I didn't know about that. I must tell George that I now know all the secrets of his ill-spent youth." The women laughed companionably together, as Mary led the way into a pleasantly shaded sitting room where tea was laid out. A young woman in a maid's uniform was waiting by the tray.

"This is Pamela, Annie," Mary Parker explained, "and I bet you can't tell me where she is from."

"Oh, yes I can, Mary," Annie pretended to think deeply, her finger to her cheek while winking at the young woman. "Ah yes! I can now definitely say: she has the stamp of one definite place; let me see, could it be St Mary's Orphanage and Girls' Home at The Junction?"

Monica clapped her hands. "There, I told you Mary, Annie's a detective!"

"Detective, my foot," laughed Annie, "I've met Pamela when I've been visiting Mother Benedicta. That's so, isn't it dear?" Pamela dropped a little curtsy and blushed.

"Are you well, Pamela? You look blooming and you're fortunate in being in such a lovely home as this."

"Yes, Mrs Watson, it's beautiful and I like it very much." Pamela blushed again and turned to her mistress. "Mrs Parker, do you wish me to stay to hand things around, or would you prefer I left?"

"No, you run along, dear. We'll manage. Thank you Pamela."

Pamela left the three women and hurried back to the kitchen. Little did she know that as soon as her back was turned, Mary Parker leaned towards her guest and said softly: "Annie, I'm worried about that dear girl. Mrs Thompson, our cook, a good and decent woman, asked me the other day if I could get John to make some enquiries about a young man she has met? I thought you might be able to have a little talk with her, if you would, before you leave today?"

Annie sighed. "It's a terrible risk, isn't it, sending the girls out from the Home? Yet what else can be done? Sister Mary Thomas, and her helpers, try their hardest to find good places for the girls, but there are so many girls. Then, there is the lure of big money in the munition factories and the so-called glamour of the city; both are so often too much to cope with, after such a sheltered upbringing."

"And," added Monica, "this is a dangerous area for a young, inexperienced girl isn't it Mary?"

"It certainly is. My own daughter, Jean, very nearly came to grief when she became infatuated with a rich, but handsome wastrel. Thank Heavens she came to her senses in time. We were very lucky, I think." Mary paused.

"But, about Pamela, Annie. I really don't know how to approach her. She could simply tell me to mind my own business – she's not a daughter. And, to tell the truth, I'd hate to lose her, she's the best maid we've ever had."

Annie jabbed two more bobby pins in her hair, as she answered.

"Thank you, Mary, for telling me. I'll certainly talk with her if that's what you wish. I'll be going on from here on Saturday morning to the Home. I will naturally see Mother Benedicta, my aunt, so if there's anything to tell her, I can do it then."

28

Annie was seated at the kitchen table with the cook and Pamela, who were having their own afternoon tea. Peggy had cooked some pikelets and insisted that Annie try them. She pronounced them delicious and asked for the recipe to take home with her.

Slowly Annie manoeuvred the conversation round to Pamela.

"I'll be seeing Mother Benedicta on Saturday, Pamela," she said, "and I'll be staying for a couple of days at the convent. I'm looking forward to it; I can't remember the last time when I've been able to get away for a few days."

"Do you have children, Mrs Watson?" asked Peggy, busy writing the recipe Annie had requested.

"Indeed, I do," Annie quickly responded. "I have a grown up daughter, Penelope, who was recently married just a few weeks ago, and a sick son who's hoping to go to University, if he can win a scholarship this year. That's why I am at home all the time."

Annie reached for another pikelet. "These are absolutely scrumptious! As I was saying, this time, I managed to get another cousin, who the kids call 'Dithering Dotti,' who's slightly crackers, but very nice, really. She's looking after everything at home for me just for a few days."

Annie began to laugh infectiously. "Poor Dorothy; she'll drive my poor husband, Sam, crazy and my boy likewise. Once, she put the cat in the fridge and the milk on the doorstep. Luckily, Billy, my son, found out in time. The cat's never been the same since!"

The cook and Pamela looked startled, then laughed along with their guest. Annie reached out and took the young girl's hand. "Did you tell Mrs Thompson, Pamela, of the time I tried to teach a group of you how to make toffee?"

Pamela started to laugh helplessly. "I see that you do remember," Annie added ruefully. "Well I didn't intend to get it all over poor Sister Clare!"

Pamela turned to the cook. "Mrs Thompson, Mrs Watson told us she was the world's best toffee maker – I don't think she'd ever made it in her life before!"

"She certainly hadn't," Annie assured her. "I had no idea that it could cause such a mess."

"And do you know what, Mrs Thompson," continued Pamela laughing, "we had toffee everywhere and Sister Clare came to help. Soon, she had her veil and her guimp – her big white starched collar – all stuck together ..."

"And, Pamela," reminded Annie, "remember how she tried to be cross and spoilt it all by collapsing with laughter before rushing to the bathroom?" They laughed happily at the memory. Annie then added, "Well, it taught me never to pretend that I was a good cook ever again. I had to apologize to Mother Benedicta as well.

"She ordered me to try to get the wretched stuff out of poor Sister Clare's veil, which didn't go very well as I had forgotten that I had it all over my hands at the time.

"When I had to face Mother Benedicta again, she was not overly impressed when I told her that I had turned one of her nuns into a large piece of toffee."

Annie looked at her watch. "Heavens, I'll have to hurry. Now, Pamela, anything to tell Mother? Job is good? You like the place and are happy here? What about young men? You must have met someone now you are living in the big city." Pamela blushed again. Mrs Thompson pretended that she had to attend to things on the stove, so excused herself from the table.

Pamela lowered her voice. "Yes, Mrs Watson, I've met a young man. I like him a lot, but there's something very mysterious about him."

"Um?"

"Well, he took me to meet his mother …"

"Really, that's usually a good sign."

"That's what I thought, but his poor mother seems to me to be a mental case; she was trying to warn me against her own son."

Annie's face wrinkled with worry. "In what way, Pamela? Just describe to me what happened when you met the mother."

Annie listened intently as Pamela recounted her meeting with Mrs Falconi. Pretty weird, Annie thought. Why's the chap not working? She decided to ask.

"Pamela, does he have a job; is he working?"

"Oh, yes, he told me about that; it's something in the government."

"I see, and does he have friends that you have met."

"Well, there's a very nice lady called Sarah Bellows who manages a very high class Club. Lucky took me to meet her as well."

"Lucky?"

"Yes, that's what he's called. His real name is Francis Falconi. He's a Catholic too, and was very respectful when he spoke of nuns as well."

Annie thought he sounded more suspicious by the minute. She stood up. "Well, I've got to go, Monica is waiting for me. Pamela, perhaps you could bring your young friend up to the Convent to meet Mother Benedicta; I know she'd like to meet him."

"I'd like that too, Mrs Watson. I'll see what he says." A bell rang from upstairs. "Excuse me, Mrs Watson, that's my bell. I must go. It's been lovely to see you again." She hurried away. Annie turned to the cook.

"What to you think, Peggy?" she asked.

"I think he's a crook, that's what I think," she answered frankly. "I've asked John – that's John Parker – to try to find out a bit about him. I'll let you know, Mrs Watson, if I hear anything."

Annie thanked the middle-aged woman and hurried to her cousin, Monica, who was waiting for her patiently upstairs. Annie was worried and troubled. There is something wrong here, and that young child is, unknowingly, at the very centre of the problem.

Falconi, Falconi ... why ... *that's* the same name ... of that strange Italian woman who came to Monica's place and acted so queerly! She said that her son was *dead*!

29

At eleven o'clock on Friday night, Lucky drove the little grey van, now sporting big signs proclaiming itself to be the 'Acme Messenger Service," down under the Sydney Town Hall, to the special place reserved for security vehicles. He showed his authority card and his licence to the guard in charge, went to the stairs indicated, and was soon at the back of the stage, where the counters were completing the final count.

Lucky identified himself, standing respectfully to one side, until the men and women were ready for him. He then signed the receipt for the heavy bag of money, said good night and was gone from the Town Hall by half past eleven.

He drove straight back to the Falcon who was waiting for him in his rooms. Lucky handed over the bag; the Falcon reminded him what he had to do the next morning; Lucky nodded, then going down to his own apartment, took off his fancy uniform, set his clock for 6.00am, and was in bed asleep within fifteen minutes. The first part of the job was over – it had been a breeze.

30

Saturday

Saturday morning dawned bright and cloudless, warm with the promise of great heat to come. Lucky mentally shrugged as he donned his ridiculous uniform. He grumbled – I wonder where the hell they got this little number from? It's ridiculous!

Before eight o'clock he was well on his way again to the Orphanage at The Junction, after collecting the bag from upstairs. The bag now felt suspiciously empty.

Arriving at the Convent, he rang the bell at the gate and spoke cheerfully and respectfully to the aged nun who faced him. He handed over the bag, asked for and received her signature to acknowledge that the money had been officially received, smiled, said good bye and was back on the road again within nine minutes. An hour later he was back home. He ripped off the 'musical comedy' uniform, and went back to bed for a couple of hours more sleep. The job was over!

31

Telephone call to Annie Watson from Mother Benedicta.

"Yes Aunt, I'm here. What on earth's the matter? I know something's wrong otherwise you would not be ringing me here at Monica's ... WHAT? You've been robbed? Tell me what happened ... bags have been altered, you think? About how much? ... Good God! Two thousand pounds! That's a fortune! ...You rang Inspector Peters? But it's not his jurisdiction ... I see, he said to contact me ... Just wait till I catch him! Well, I can understand what the loss of so much money means to you with all your waifs to feed, but why are you so distressed? The police will find the culprits and...

"WHAT? No! That's not possible! You think one of the Sisters is involved in some way? ...Merciful God ... Yes, I *do* understand, Aunt; that is terrible! An inside job! It's hard to believe! ...Yes, I was just about to leave here ... No, I'll come as quickly as I can – should be there in about one hour ... Well, I'll try, Aunt ... but, be reasonable; I'm not a detective, I may not be able to do anything ... Well, those other times were different ... We'll see. Bye."

32

Annie Watson put down her suitcase on the pavement and pushed the bell on the heavy wooden gate leading into the sprawling complex of St Mary's Orphanage and Girls' Home. The top half of the door opened inward and an aged nun's face broke into happy smiles as she recognized the visitor.

"Miss Anne," she cried as she undid the lower locks of the door, "come in; come in. Mother told us you were coming. I was so looking forward to seeing you again."

Annie entered the doorway and kissed the elderly nun. "Sister Agatha, I see you are still guarding the gates like St Peter." The nun laughed; her small wrinkled face lighting up while her shrewd eyes behind their thick spectacles looked closely at Annie.

"You know, Miss Anne, as you grow older, you look more and more like your wonderful mother – I'm so glad you've never cut your hair, or had it permed in those dreadful tight curls that women seem to think fashionable today. With your hair up, you look even more like Lady Mary."

"I've often thought of taking the scissors and cutting it all off," Annie admitted, "it's a damn nuisance and is always falling down, but I'm used to it. I really can't be bothered with fashion; I always get it wrong anyhow. I'm the despair of my daughter, Penny, she thinks I look like a rag-bag."

Annie came closer to the old nun and spoke softly. "How is she,

Sister? Before I left this morning, she rang me about the robbery. I could hardly believe it. It must have been a horrendous shock to her?"

"It was, Annie. Mother cannot believe it has happened, either – an actual theft in this place and … what a theft! And, then to think that it could have been … what is that police expression?"

"An inside job."

"Yes that's it." Sister Agatha put her gnarled fingers on Annie's arm. "Mother's not young anymore; she worries non-stop about everybody in this place, and, now to have this!" Sister Agatha closed her eyes in horror.

"Mother called a special Chapter meeting, when the theft was discovered, to tell us all about it. I thought, while I was listening to her, that she looked ten years older. She had to notify the police and they were the ones who said it must be an inside job. God help us!"

The nun moved back into her little shelter. "Miss Anne, go on up; she's expecting you. Please God you'll get to the bottom of this. I'll pray for you down here at the gate."

Annie smiled and, taking her case, moved away towards the stairs to her right. She paused as she stood at the foot of the stairs looking at the little separate world that was the institution.

Annie, having visited Mother Benedicta countless times, was familiar with the place, but had never really considered how difficult it must be to make the whole thing work.

The food alone would be a nightmare. It was a daunting thought. Her eyes were caught by a nun bringing out a group of very young children, boys and girls, for some physical exercises. The nun was wearing sandshoes and the older girls were carrying balls and skipping ropes and other equipment. There was a happy burst of giggling and laughing.

That's the Infants school kids, Annie thought, there must be about thirty of them; there's also the middle and senior school, about another thirty girls – could be more.

Then there are those who are finished school and waiting to find work – a sudden thought wrinkled Annie's brow: those girls are permitted to go out in pairs to entertainments, or for interviews for work; they could have met bad people, or simply gossiped – I must keep them in mind. Who else is here? The precious little ones in the nursery, Annie smiled tenderly. I wonder how many are there now. It usually was about fifteen or twenty, but the number changed constantly.

And finally, she pondered sadly, there are the girls who have come back here because of some misfortune – losing their position, getting into bad company, and even some who had been in gaol, who had nowhere else to go.

Annie knew Mother Benedicta employed them in the kitchen and in the laundry, or at least as many as she could, but they were usually kept separate from the school age children – that must be hard on them, but it could well be necessary. But, even if that were the rule, it would require some doing to enforce it, Annie thought.

How many are actually here altogether that have to be cared for, she wondered; must be about 100, or more, counting the nuns themselves. She remembered there are twenty four nuns including the five, very elderly ones, who mainly work in the kitchen preparing the huge mound of vegetables each day, assisting with the washing-up or helping with the endless folding of clothes in the laundry.

Finally, there was dear old Sister Agatha, the Portress, at the gate – tiny, strong as an ox, but with twinkling eyes that could still see the world with humour, and with great compassion.

Annie began to climb the stairs slowly, casting her mind back to her Aunt's phone call. Benedicta had told her all she herself knew of the details of the problem. A big Charity had donated their annual Ball and Auction night proceeds to St Mary's. The nun in charge of the moneys in this place had given the organizer a carpet bag which could be locked when the money had been placed inside.

The nun had left the bag unlocked and kept the key in her own possession. The bag was self-locking and after the actual notes and coins had been counted and placed in it, the bag had then been duly locked by the Charity workers after the event was over.

The counters had handed the bag to a delivery man from the Acme Messenger Service, which they claimed the finance nun had specified; it had duly been delivered to the Convent this morning early.

There seemed to be some problem in deciding why it was not opened immediately. However, when it was opened, it contained some coins, but the rest was only massed bundles of bound pieces of newspaper cut in the shape of bank notes.

Annie had almost reached the top of the stairs when she realised that Sister Agatha would have seen the delivery man. Leaving her suitcase there, she hastily retraced her steps and questioned the old nun.

"Indeed, I did see him, Miss Anne," Sister Agatha answered promptly.

"Sister, I know you of old. You wouldn't be in this vitally important position guarding the gate, seeing all who enter and leave this place, if you didn't have the eyes of a hawk and notice every-thing, so tell me, could you describe the man?"

The nun looked surprised. "Of course, Miss Anne. He was about twenty-two or twenty-four years of age, not very tall, about five foot nine or ten, had dark hair – a little longer than is usual, and a thin moustache. His eyes were dark and rather large while his lips were a surprisingly rosy colour while his skin was sallow – I suspect there was Italian blood somewhere in his make-up."

Annie began to laugh. "What a blessing you would be to the police force, Sister. That was magnificent. Now, don't disappoint me, tell me what he was wearing?"

"You're laughing at me, Miss Anne, I know," the nun replied, her eyes twinkling in amusement. "However, I can tell you that. He had on a uniform; it was dark blue in colour with silver buttons on the jacket. It had a stiff collar – the jacket, I mean – and had some kind of braid on it. I thought, at the time, that it was rather a 'theatrical' kind of uniform – something that I've heard ushers use in cinemas.

"I just wondered why that firm dressed up their men in such a fancy outfit."

"You must have had to sign for the bag, Sister?"

"Certainly. This young man produced an ordinary receipt book, and I read quickly what was written, and then signed my name. As I thought the bag would be heavy, I opened the lower part of the door and asked the man to put the bag on the floor.

"The strange thing was, that after he had jumped into the van – before you ask me, it was a small grey van with the name of the firm on the side in large letters – I bent to see if I could lift the bag to take it upstairs and I found it to be very light. I thought that must be because the money must be all in notes. I rang through to Sister Josepha – our finance nun – and she came down immediately and took possession of the bag."

"One last question, Sister. Did the delivery man speak much? Was he rude, or unpleasant?"

"Exactly the opposite! It was 'Sister this,' and 'Sister that' and leaving he said: 'Bless you Sister, pray for me', and if you want my opinion of him Miss Anne, I'll tell you: I wouldn't trust him an inch. He'd try to sell you the Sydney Harbour Bridge."

Annie laughed with genuine amusement. She hugged the elderly woman briefly and then ran up the stairs to her Aunt's office.

33

Annie stood at the door of her aunt's office noticing that it was even more hopelessly untidy than usual. Her aunt's dumpty figure was standing slumped over, near her little fire place, her elbow resting on the mantelpiece holding her chin in her hand. She did not notice Annie arrive.

Annie knew well, when Mother Benedicta did become aware of her niece, her veil would be askew and she would tug her stiffly starched guimp back into place, with an irritated pull, if it was out of kilter. She wore half glasses which always slipped down her nose; her cheeks were usually slightly flushed, but were now drained of colour. Her fine eyes with startlingly blue pupils were staring at nothing; her lips moving silently.

Annie realised that her aunt was still in shock at what had happened.

The troubled nun became aware of the figure standing in the doorway. She moved rapidly towards Annie and folded her silently in a huge embrace. She led Annie to one of the two chairs before the empty fire place.

She had not uttered one word. She tried to clear her throat and began to speak. Normally she was a rapid speaker, requiring the listener to pay close attention to follow her; now she spoke hesitantly, her voice muffled with emotion. She spoke tremulously.

"Annie, I knew you were on your way; so much for the little holiday you thought you would be having. To have to walk into this! But I'm so very grateful you're here." Annie took her aunt's hands and warmed them within her own.

"Well, here I am, the eternal busybody and all I can say is: Here's a fine How-de-do!"

"Annie," Mother Benedicta said, "this whole affair is such a delicate one. I didn't really know whom I *could* consult. As soon as the theft was discovered, I rang Inspector Peters immediately; the problem is that he can't really take over the investigation – it's not his area, as you mentioned on the phone. He advised me whom I must contact here at The Junction, but he gave me the hint – to be fair, he couldn't do more; it's a criminal matter – to get in touch with you. He was relieved when I told him you were on your way here for a visit today."

"But I'm still in the dark, Aunt," Annie replied, "about all the details. You hinted that one of the Sisters was helping the police with their enquiries. Is that the case?"

"Yes, it is. God forgive me, if I'm wrong, but I think it's the truth, Annie," whispered the elderly woman. "I would like to think I know the members of my own community; I've lived with most of them for many, many years in this place. But this, this…"

The elderly nun pushed her half-moon glasses up her nose absent-mindedly and continued: "I think one of them has deceived me. I think she's a thief!"

"And is the amount really two thousand pounds?"

"Roughly about that, Annie," the Mother Superior actually wrung her hands. "Dear God, what am I to do?"

"Mercifully Heavens! It's a fortune to me!"

"It's not a fortune here where we have over 100 mouths to feed three times a day; this donation would have been such a wonderful help."

"Well, as the police know you have received the fake money from the messenger, I suppose everyone knows now. I guess the police informed the press."

"Oh yes, Annie," Mother Benedicta lifted her troubled plump face to her niece and smiled briefly. "There's no hope of hiding the scandal; it's all out in the open now."

"It doesn't make sense. I've spoken to Sister Agatha – she was very helpful. Did you, or any of the Sisters, insist the Charity use that particular messenger service?"

"I certainly didn't; I'd never heard of it, and who else would have done it except Sister Josepha. She's the nun who looks after all the money that comes in to keep this place going. She and her assistant, Sister Mary Margaret, do all the banking, but Sister Josepha organises all the details. She also is the only one who is in contact with the committees of various fund-raising Charities."

"How long has Sister Josepha been a nun?"

"It must be fifteen years, I think. She's about thirty-five or six."

"And, how long has she been here under your care and taking control of the money?"

"The same length of time. When I was given this place to run, I made it clear I needed someone trained in finance to help me. Believe me, to try to keep this place going and to keep 100 mouths fed, needs not only faith, but a financial machine to keep it rolling.

"We have wonderful help from individual people; big and small donations come in every day, thank God and, of course, there's the special collections made in the big Churches. We need every bit of help we can get just to keep going. This big donation would have been a great blessing to us now, in this time of war."

"So, to help you with your 'financial machine' they sent you Sister Mary Josepha."

"Yes, although Sister Josepha trained as a nurse, she also was brilliant at financial administration; working for a time at Lewisham

Hospital in the finance section. They also sent Sister Mary Margaret; she did actually work in a bank before becoming a nun."

"What is Sister Josepha like?"

"A good, quiet, hard-working nun, well liked by the community; not bossy, no pretence about her, serious, yet always pleasant, quietly spoken."

"Do you like her?" interrupted Annie.

"What's that got to do with it? I am the Mother Superior, Annie. Every one of these women call me 'Mother.' Does a Mother make distinctions between her children? Does she *like* this one, or not like that one…"

"She does, actually. I see, so you don't actually like her, do you?"

Mother Benedicta, as well as being a highly intelligent and educated nun, was also a very honest person. Perplexed by her niece's perception, she rubbed her nose with vexation. After a pause she admitted:

"Well, if you *must* know, if I was faced with having to select one member of the community to keep me company in exile on a desert island, Sister Josepha would not be the one I would choose."

"Why?"

"Why do you persist in this line of questioning, Annie? It's difficult enough for me as it is."

"Because it *is* important. You are not a young fresh-faced nun filled with the wonder of her calling, oblivious to everything, other than her spiritual duties. You are a shrewd and tough old bird, from a long line of shrewd, tough old birds.

"What I mean is: you've had enormous experience in dealing with every kind of female in your care for nearly forty years. If you think there's a possibility there's something wrong, you can be pretty sure there is."

The Mother Superior thought about Annie's answer. Finally, she said, "I can't pretend that I haven't had plenty of experience dealing with women of all kinds, but in this particular place, I simply don't have the time to spend on the community that I should. I have too many other responsibilities."

"Surely you have an Assistant?"

"I do, Sister Mary Michael, my right hand. She is a gift from Heaven. She tries to lift the burden and certainly does so; she is totally competent. One of her main duties is to see that I *know* everything that's going on – and that means with all the girls as well as the community."

There was a little knock on the door and a pleasant voice called out: "Benedicite, Mother."

The Superior replied: "Deus, Sister," and turned to Annie. "Excuse me a moment, Annie."

A vigorous nun in her mid-thirties came into the room, paused uncertainly, and bowed slightly to Annie. She led in another nun who hesitantly pulled back, seeing the visitor, remaining near the door. Annie looked at the second nun and involuntarily gasped – which she tried desperately to turn into a cough.

The Superior introduced the Sisters to Annie. "Annie, this is another wonderful member of our community, Sister Mary Thomas – she's the one who searches everywhere for jobs for our girls, browbeats employers to find work for them, then goes and checks them out to see if they're genuine or not … and this is Sister Mary Luke."

Benedicta's voice changed; it became uneven. She cleared her throat and then spoke heartily. "She's the best music teacher we've ever had. Sisters, this is my niece, Mrs Anne Watson."

Mother Benedicta swept on: "Now, what have you found, Sister Thomas – I know that look of old."

"Believe it or not, Mother, this morning we've had the offer of places for no less than six of our girls – two office jobs in a good, respectable firm and four requests for maids in good homes. I have an interview with the manager of the office this morning and as I know where this place is, I had an idea.

"There's a small park next to the place and I thought, if you agree, I'd take Sister Luke with me. We could have a little walk in the park after the interview. There are ducks in the park and we could take some stale bread from the kitchen …"

"Permission gladly given, but Sister, *please*, just a little walk, *promise* me … and you must take another nun with you; you might need assistance. See if Sister Clare or Sister Raphael is free for a couple of hours."

"I understand Mother. I'll take the car, as it's free, so we won't be long away."

Benedicta turned to the silent nun. "Are you happy to go on this outing, my dear child?"

Sister Luke smiled and answered softly, "I would love it, my lady Mother."

The elderly nun took out her handkerchief and blew her nose loudly. "Then off you two gad-a-bouts go. I don't know what nuns are coming to these days … walking in parks, feeding ducks …" She waved her hand in dismissal. The Sisters, smiling, left the room.

Annie reached out and patted her Aunt's hand. "Merciful God, Aunt, what is wrong with the thin nun? Her skin is transparent parchment; she is merely skin and bones. Her eyes are enormous… and her cheekbones! Dear God, she looks like death."

"That's exactly what it is you're seeing, Annie. My poor, precious, Sister Luke, is dying of an inoperable cancer. She has only a couple of months left, the doctors tell me." Benedicta dabbed angrily at her eyes. "How old do you think she is, Annie?"

"Old? Well, I got such a shock when I saw her. I'm not sure – about thirty-five, forty, maybe."

"She's twenty-four! She's Sir Henry Walker's daughter: their only child. I offered to let her go home if she wanted to, but she begged to stay. The only thing she requested was to be able to make her final vows.

"I had to get permission for that from the bishop as she's under age, but under the circumstances, it was given – she'll die a fully perpetually professed nun. That's something, anyhow."

Benedicta sighed and turned again to Annie. "You see, Annie, I simply don't have the time to concentrate on stupid burglaries. Nuns like Sister Luke are too precious and too few. Oh, dear God, our faith is tested and tested isn't it?"

"I don't know how you manage it at all. It's a family the size of a small army you are looking after, or a town. Yes, that's it. This place is like a little town, all within its own walls."

Annie stood up. "Right! Let's get this wretched burglary sorted out. Back to where we were. Tell me honestly now, why are you uncertain about Sister Josepha?"

"She is secretive, Annie. A good nun, on the whole, is a happy, usually out-going, easy to read person. Josepha is *not*; she is always reserved. To my mind it's unnatural. Look for an actual fault; it would be hard to find one, but always you feel, when talking to her, that she is hiding a part of herself – that she is playing a part. But that's ridiculous. She's been a nun for fifteen years."

Benedicta pushed herself out of her chair and stood up, her short dumpy figure hidden by the black voluminous clothes.

"You know, Annie, the whole problem with Josepha could simply be, that I happen to like people who are open, easy to be with, easy to lead, as well as to read. Perhaps she really has a secret in her past; that'd be no problem for me.

"I'm not so naïve as to imagine that every girl that God calls to this life has not things in her past that only her Confessor and she know about. That is between God and the nun, and nothing to do with me and wouldn't worry me either. God knows what He is doing in that regard."

The elderly nun gave Annie a sharp look. "Annie, go and see Sister Josepha; tell her I sent you, and ask her to explain about the money. And, while you're doing it you can make up your mind about the woman yourself.

"And," the elderly woman added, raising her eyebrows significantly, "if I am, as you so rudely said, a tough old bird, let me remind you that, of all the family, you are said to resemble me the most!"

Annie smiled, gave her aunt a quick kiss on the cheek, and went out the door in quest of the 'finance' nun, Sister Mary Josepha.

34

Sister Josepha had a small office to herself. She was working on a pile of papers when Annie knocked on the open door. The nun smiled, rose and beckoned the visitor to a chair. Annie studied the nun closely.

She was a tall nun, matching Annie in height, her cheeks were slightly flushed but her skin was alabaster white. Her eyes were dark and sombre but very beautiful, fringed with long black lashes, which matched her finely shaped eyebrows.

Her facial expression had appeared anxious, when Annie first observed her, but as soon as the nun was aware of the visitor, it resumed its placid and unemotional, tranquil appearance.

She appeared to be about thirty or thirty-five years of age. Annie noticed the nun's hands; the fingers were beautiful; long and thin and delicately shaped. She spoke quietly and with dignity.

'Please sit down, Mrs Watson. Mother Benedicta informed us at Chapter meeting that you would be coming here to see us; she told me, especially, to be ready to receive you.'

Annie extended her hand; the nun looked surprised, but hastily shook hands and then remained standing, her hands back in her wide sleeves, until Annie had been seated. She then sat, straight and still, waiting for Annie to begin the questions.

"I'm glad Mother Benedicta has spoken to the community about me being here," Annie began. "It makes it easier for me not having to explain myself everywhere I go." She shrugged her shoulders expressively and spoke ruefully. "I can imagine the wild stories that are already circulating about me."

Josepha permitted herself a small smile. "Well, Mrs Watson, you are fairly famous you know, what with murders while nearly getting yourself killed. Some of the Sisters call you Mother Benedicta's famous detective niece."

Annie laughed. "If they believe that, they'll believe anything. Anyhow," Annie sat up and attempted to tidy her hair, "that's neither here nor there. Tell me Sister about the theft of the money."

"I know I'm under suspicion," Josepha answered. "I don't really know what I should do?"

"Sister, if you are in any way involved in the matter – which I find difficult to believe – that is between you and Mother Benedicta; not with me. I am not your Confessor, so let's start on another track. Tell me what you do here at the Home."

"As you now probably know, I deal with all the moneys coming into this place. It comes from so many sources that it is quite a big job keeping track of it all. You would also know that every donation is acknowledged, even the smallest, so that keeps two senior girls and me, very busy.

"The girls are excellent typists and write the 'thank-you' notes. The small amounts are often a nuisance: keeping track of them all – dreadfully needed as they are – but it is the really big donations that have to be watched very carefully."

The nun paused and stared briefly into space. "Besides the two girl typists, I have Sister Mary Margaret as my assistant. She worked in a bank and is a godsend to me, as she can count and wrap coins at the speed of light, which I can't."

"I can imagine that'd be a great help," agreed Annie. "Tell me about the two thousand pounds donation step by step. I know about the bag."

"I gave the bag to the organizer before the Charity event – I don't know what it was. He told me this morning – on the phone – he put all the proceeds of the function into the bag, *after* the event, last night; the bag was closed – it is self-locking – and was handed to a Security Firm. I believe the name is the 'Acme Messenger Service'. The bag was tagged with my name and brought by the messenger service to the gate very early this morning. It was then handed in to Sister Agatha, the Portress, who signed a receipt for it.

"She called me down to bring it up here; she thought it might be too heavy for her, as she is an elderly nun. I should then have locked it in the huge safe in Mother Benedicta's office. That is the normal procedure. It is taken, with any other moneys, to the Bank by Sister Margaret and me – with the assistance of my two young helpers."

The nun raised her eyes. "Mrs Watson, I have a driving licence and I drive the Convent car to the Bank."

"I see. So if the money – in the carpet bag – didn't go into the safe, where did it go?"

"I was about to take it to the safe, when I was called away to an accident. One of the small Primary School girls had cut her foot quite badly and as I am a trained nurse and was closest to the area, the Sister in charge, sent a girl from sixth grade to get me in a hurry.

"Among the Sisters here, there are six qualified Nursing Sisters – trained at Lewisham Hospital – and they are much younger than I. As soon as I saw how serious the cut was, I sent for one of the other nuns, a Sister Raphael – she had finished her medical degree before entering the convent and knows much more than I do.

"It took me a little while to attend to the matter. I stopped the flow of blood, but realised that the wound would have to be stitched – the medical nun could do that. As soon as Sister Mary Raphael arrived, I came back in here to continue the task I had been about to do."

"Was the money bag still in the same position as when you left it?"

"Yes, it seemed to be exactly as it was before. But it wasn't …"

"Explain."

"I happened to notice that the clasp was loose. It is an old bag and I was not unduly worried; but when I opened it …"

"Yes?"

For the first time, the nun's composure started to unravel. Annie noticed that her hands were trembling within her wide sleeves. Without raising her eyes, she continued.

"I opened the bag and couldn't believe my eyes. There were bundles of notes still there, but they were all carefully cut …bundles … of … newspaper. There were only a few coins at the bottom of the case – everything else was paper!"

"What did you do?

"I was so shocked I don't know exactly what I did. I remember looking around the office – which was a ridiculous thing to do. Gradually, the truth sank in that we had been robbed."

The nun paused. "I then had to take the bag of newspapers to our Mother Superior." Sister Josepha's voice shook a little; she shut her eyes completely for a few seconds and then, with an obvious mental struggle, raised her head and looked straight at Annie.

"Mrs Watson, I don't know how it happened, or why it happened, when it did. I simply don't understand it at all."

"But you would have noticed that the bag was strangely light wouldn't you, when you picked it up," Annie asked.

"I suppose I did, but it didn't register. I most probably expected that it would be paper money – all notes – but, to be honest, I don't think I even thought of it at all. I handle a great deal of money in this position."

"Tell me Sister, did you happen to see the man who delivered the bag to Sister Agnes?"

Annie was surprised at the result of this question. There was a long silence and she noticed that Sister Josepha's right hand, which she had moved from her sleeve to lean on her desk, suddenly was clenched so tight that all the knuckles were visible. She closed her eyes and answered slowly and reluctantly.

"Only a quick glance. He was leaving as I arrived at the gate."

"And?"

Sister Josepha now spoke quickly, rattling off the description. "He was a middle-aged man, very tall, with light coloured hair. He wore glasses and was wearing a grey suit."

Annie remained silent looking at the woman in front of her. The nun was so still she could easily have been mistaken for a piece of sculpture. Annie wondered. Why had the woman so deliberately lied? It obviously cost her greatly to utter those lies, yet she had deliberately done so.

"Sister, what about the messenger service? Is it the usual firm you employ? Where does it come from?"

Now the nun's voice became slightly breathless. "No, we do not use that firm; this was the first time."

"How did you come to use it this time? Why did you, personally, recommend it?"

The nun became so tense, Annie was worried. Something was going to happen soon she knew. She quickly decided to go on to another subject, not giving the nun the time to think up another lie, for Annie guessed whatever this poor distraught woman said next would be a fabrication.

"Sister, forget the robbery, for a moment. Tell me about yourself. For some reason your face looks familiar. I think I must have seen you before, or met you before, or met your parents or ..."

The effect of Annie's words was electric. Sister Josepha leapt to her feet, her hands now clenched at her sides. Her voice was like ice, her face a blank mask. Each word she spoke was hissed through her teeth.

"My parents! How dare you! Leave my parents alone. You know nothing about me; you have never met me before; you have no right whatsoever to question me about anything. Before God, only Mother Benedicta and the police have that right. I refuse absolutely to answer another question from you." Sister Josepha moved agitatedly to the door of her office. "Excuse me, I must go to the Chapel."

So saying, Sister Josepha hurried quickly through the door and Annie heard her actually running along the corridor towards the Chapel. It also sounded as if Sister Josepha was sobbing loudly and uncontrollably.

Weirder and weirder, mused Annie, slowly rising to her feet. So Josepha is definitely involved. She knew the bag was empty; she knows the man who delivered the phoney bag of money and it was she who obviously arranged to use this 'Acme' firm, which, I'll bet my bottom dollar, no longer exists.

But why? The money was useless to the nun – she couldn't spend it, nor would she ever see it. Why was it important for her to lie? It obviously unnerved her to do so. There was something terribly wrong here, and it would be so easy at this point to make a gigantic mistake.

Annie sighed, stood up and prepared to go to the office next door to see the girls and Josepha's assistant, Sister Mary Margaret. She was nearly there when she remembered something and hurried back to Mother Benedicta's office.

35

There was a short, grey haired man talking with the Superior when Annie charged into the office. She stopped suddenly, her eyes wide with surprise. "Well, I was just thinking of you, Inspector Peters; lo and behold, here you are!"

Annie turned to her Aunt. "Forgive me, Aunt, for rushing in; I didn't know you were being interrogated by the police! Promise me you won't arrest her, Inspector."

Annie smiled and shook hands with the Inspector. They knew each other well as Annie had been involved with many of Inspector Peters' cases, ever since the first tragic event in Bexford North had brought them together. They had come, not only to respect each other, but to be at ease together.

"Annie, just keep quiet for a moment, will you?" demanded Mother Benedicta brusquely. "Listen to what I had to tell Inspector Peters. This will surprise you. Truly this case gets stranger by the minute."

Annie sat down, puzzled, and turned expectantly to the nun. Mother Benedicta was disturbed; her usual placid face clearly indicating her bewilderment. "I should be dancing for joy, I suppose, Annie, but it's all so … puzzling."

"For heaven's sake, Aunt, *what* is?" The nun looked helplessly at the policeman. He took over.

"Mrs Watson, strange as it may be to believe, Mother Benedicta received a call from an agitated woman a little while ago, telling her the robbery was all a joke that went wrong; all the money would be returned tomorrow morning. She was also told to inform the police of the arrangements."

"WHAT!" Annie stood up in her shock. "You're kidding me Inspector!"

"Truly, I'm not." Peters shook his head. 'It doesn't make sense. There was no 'joke' about it; it was all carefully planned and carried out."

"But what could be the explanation of the call, Inspector?" the Mother Superior asked.

Annie intervened before Peters could speak. "Could it be that one of the gang has fallen out, or had scruples, or is just afraid at all the publicity and is ratting on his fellow criminals? There must have been others involved in this; it was too well planned and executed, even down to the fake delivery van."

"What you have just said is the only solution that makes any sense at all, Mrs Watson," agreed the Inspector, "or, at least, the only one I could think of."

"Where do we stand, now Inspector?" Mother Benedicta asked. "As it seems that one of my Community, Sister Josepha, was involved, what is her position now? Is she still in danger of being charged?"

"Well, if she was involved, or any others, that we do not know about, then, technically, they could be charged with being accessories before the crime or, even with simply perverting the cause of Justice by wasting the time of the police." Benedicta winced and closed her eyes.

"However, I've had a word with Inspector West, here at The Junction. Both he and I, are of the opinion that, if there is a satisfactory explanation by the nun, or nuns involved, then it could easily be dismissed by the magistrate." Peters thinking over what he had just said, realised that it needed clarification.

"You see, if it could be shown that the nun was aiding the

criminals through coercion, or through fear – for herself, or, for others – then it could become merely a minor offence."

"I suppose, Inspector, it really means waiting for tomorrow morning to see if the money *is* actually returned," Annie summed up. "It is possible that the recent phone call was a hoax in itself."

"For the love of God, don't say that, Annie," Mother Benedicta cried. "I don't think I could bear any more of this."

"Well, Aunt, we have to face all the possibilities – there's no easy way out of this one."

Inspector Peters stood up preparing to leave.

"I think you've summed up the gist of the matter, Mrs Watson. I think we'll just have to wait and see. However, that doesn't mean the police will be stopping their investigation of the crime; it remains exactly that, until there is proof otherwise." He held out his hand to the nun.

"Mother, thank you for letting me know so quickly about the call. Inspector West has promised that he will inform me what happens tomorrow morning."

"And thank you for coming so quickly, Inspector. We are in your debt again, and all we can do to show our gratitude, is to pray for you, which, believe me, we shall do with a vengeance." Mother Benedicta shook hands vigorously.

Inspector Peters nodded to Annie and left the room. Mother Benedicta slumped back in her chair.

"You were right, Annie, what a how- to-do! I don't know whether I'm on my head or my heels," she straightened up. "All right. Now, what did you find out, and why were you rushing in here? Something must have come up."

"I'm convinced Sister Josepha is involved, but most definitely against her will. She has been coerced, by some method or other, to act as she has done. She is in great stress of mind, grieving that she has betrayed you and has gone rushing to the Chapel apparently in an agony of repentance."

Mother Benedicta made a move as if to leave the room.

"No, wait a minute. I must know something. What is her background? I've seen her somewhere before, or at least someone who is the mirror image of her. So I want to know who her parents are. We *must* know her surname. I think that's vital at the moment. Somewhere you must have her original documents – the ones she had when she applied for permission to enter the convent."

The Superior looked troubled. "Well, as I think I told you, Sister's parents are dead, I *think*, but the names would be on her original documents. The problem is they're at the Mother House and that would take days to get them sent here … Wait a minute, her surname? I've heard … It's … No, can't remember it – we never use the surname after we take the Habit … but I do have a vague recollection – it came up in something I read. I *think* it's an Italian name."

"Oh, she's Italian is she?"

"Yes, but Australian born. I remember now, I once asked her about her parents I think she told me that both were dead."

"Siblings?

"I honestly don't know."

"What about visitors."

"I've never known her to have any family visitors. She has had some women friends of the Home to visit her, but no family."

"Well, you'll have to see her. I think she wants to tell you everything herself. I tried to get information from her about her family; she went off like a rocket, refusing to tell me anything – which, of course, could be an indication that she most certainly *does* have family, and that something's wrong."

"Yes, I see. I'll go to the Chapel and try to bring her back here. You had better get out of the way, Annie. If she sees you, she'll think it's a put up job."

Annie smiled and winked. "Which, of course, it is."

"Yes, but it is better if she doesn't know that," Benedicta smiled briefly and hurried from her office.

36

The Falcon was angry. He was still fuming late Saturday morning over Sarah Bellows' phone call. It was the shock of her rebellion that infuriated him. How dare she speak to him like that! And, to *threaten Him*! She'll pay for that, the ungrateful bitch! How *dare* she? *She'll learn not to cross him again.*

He looked up impatiently as his daughter-in-law shuffled into the room from his bathroom with a bucket, a mop and a pile of dirty washing. He turned his fury onto the elderly woman.

"Hey you! Hurry up, finish and get out, you pathetic apology for a woman; you imbecilic bundle of mindless, shapeless idiocy!"

The Falcon picked up a heavy paperweight from his desk and threw it at the helpless woman, who cowered back into a corner, then shuffled out as quickly as she could from his presence.

Angelina trembled as she hurried downstairs to her own section of the house. Safe there, she looked up at the next floor, raised her two fists and shook them in the air. Angelina, having relieved her feelings, then smiled grimly.

At last she had found a way to outwit that man – that murderer! She vividly recalled the day her husband was murdered: another victim of this monster – this fiend who had made her live in terror for so many long, lonely years. Little did he know that she – the stupid, useless one – was going to destroy his plans!

What he would do if she ever found out, she refused to think. He would kill her, that's for sure, but it would be dying for something worthwhile, so what did it really matter? ...She was of no interest, no importance, to anyone.

Angelina went to the bench under the sink in her kitchen and glanced happily at the basket of potatoes hidden there. Angelina patted the potatoes gently. The Falcon would be surprised, she thought grimly, if he got the chance to look under the potatoes; after she had finished the work she planned to do on Saturday night.

Angelina knew that the Falcon regarded her as a retarded, mental defective, and usually ignored her presence at all times. He had become, over the years, so used to her silent presence that he really didn't even notice her at all. In that, he had made a terrible mistake.

Being so used to her presence, he was unguarded in his speech with others, when she was in his rooms cleaning. Ever since she had heard of his latest plans – via the dumbwaiter – regarding the robbery and the murder, Angelina's mind was capable of only one line of thought: how to thwart him.

She had been horrified to hear the *name* of the place that was to be robbed, then of the planned murder of a *nun* from the same place! At first she had just wrung her hands in panic; but as the shock subsided, she realised she *had* to actually *do* something to prevent that – there was absolutely no one else who could help.

But *what*, she had kept asking herself; then had come the simple answer. As always, the elderly woman had prayed for help, standing before her big crucifix holding the small picture of her daughter in her hands. Standing there with her daughter's photo, she prayed especially for the *courage* she would need to do what she had decided to do.

She had worked out a plan. She knew, from her listening, when the money was coming from the Charity function into the house. It would go into the Falcon's big safe late Friday night. Therefore, she knew she must get it from the safe, but she would have to leave it until *Saturday* night – after they were all asleep up there.

She had seen the Falcon open the big safe numerous times; she now stood with her eyes tightly closed thinking of the numbers he had used.

She had been interested the first time she had seen it being opened, prolonging her scrubbing, just to find out how it was done. There were five numbers, she remembered: a five, a seven, a two, an eight, and a one – yes, she was sure that was right.

In order to remember the numbers, Angelina had kept saying them over and over silently in her head: 57281.

On Saturday night, after those upstairs had gone to bed, she would act. Thank God for the dumbwaiter; this time it would be *carrying a passenger, not food!*

37

Meanwhile, upstairs, the Falcon was mulling over a plan to put a stop once and for all to the rebellion of Sarah Bellows. His vanity was outraged. *How dare she do this*?

Well, there's nothing else for it; she had to learn her lesson. Making a sudden decision he pressed the bell for his two body guards who hurried to his study.

"Listen carefully to me," he ordered. "I want a snatch done and I want you two to do it." The men looked briefly at each other, then nodded. It would make a break from just plain bodyguard work anyhow. "Who, boss?" Tarzan asked.

"A young woman called Pamela Scott. She's a maid at the Parker's big, white place in Lilac Street, Potts Point – number 28. I want it done on Sunday morning early. She's a servant and a Catholic, so she'll be off to the early Mass. Be there before six o'clock, but keep out of sight – this is a posh area as you know.

"I've been around there this morning and cased the house. I think the best way would be to go around the side of the house and down to the kitchen area. The girl will be leaving from that door, not the main one. Grab her quickly, have the car ready close by and get her into the car as quickly as you can."

"There shouldn't be too many around, Boss, at that hour on a Sunday morning," Jane observed. "What do you want done with her?"

"I want her hidden at Daphne's place. I'll ring Daphne and tell her to lock her in a room and make sure that the other girls don't see her." The Falcon looked closely at the two men. "Is that clear? Just in, grab the girl as she comes out, then into the car and back to Daphne's place. Right?"

The men nodded again. "Number 28. OK. It'll be done, Boss. Don't worry, we'll handle it properly." The Falcon looked searchingly at them again, and nodded his dismissal. They left the room.

Step one in his plan had been arranged. That would teach the upstart bitch a lesson. She won't cross the Falcon again!

38

Mother Benedicta on her way back to her office saw Annie talking with Sister Mary Margaret. She beckoned to Annie to follow her. Back in her own office, Benedicta explained her mission to the Chapel.

"I told the poor wretched nun that the money was going to be returned tomorrow morning – please God I hope that's what actually *does* happen. Sister Josepha was so overcome with that news that she cried and cried; I thought she would never stop."

Benedicta rubbed her nose in her agitation. "How on earth I ever thought that Sister was reserved I don't know! She was like a little child in her gratitude to God for the miracle of the return of the money.

"I had to caution her that it hadn't actually happened yet. But, she kept interrupting me; saying that it was a miracle; that God had heard her pleas. Really she was so distraught I suggested she go to bed and I would send Sister Raphael to give her a mild sedative. It was obvious to me that she has been under tremendous strain."

The elderly nun raised troubled eyes to Annie. "Whether it was right or wrong, I don't know, Annie, but I told her to postpone her confession of her part in the affair until after tomorrow morning. I was frightened for her sanity; I didn't know if she could take any more."

"And her surname? Did you get it?"

Mother Benedicta closed her eyes tight in vexation. "Oh, I'm an idiot. I was so distressed at her condition that I completely forgot I was supposed to question her."

She looked at Annie in distress. "Couldn't it wait until tomorrow, Annie? I truly don't think Josepha could cope with any more stress today. She has clearly been suffering silently all these years and, God forgive me, I was not aware of it."

The elderly nun let her glasses slip down her nose and rubbed her forehead gently, with her thumbs; it was obvious to Annie that Benedicta was unwell.

"Well, let's try another way, Aunt," Annie suggested. "Ring the Mother House in Bathurst. Try to get the information you need from the nun in charge of the files there. In that way you don't have to interrogate Josepha at all."

"You're a sensible woman, Annie, that's a good plan; I'll do that." Benedicta paused and, smiling slightly, raised her eyebrows knowingly. "Tell me, what was your impression of Sister Margaret?" Annie smiled, and answered without hesitation.

"I know that look, Aunt. It means that you think the same. A pain in the neck, would be the easiest way to describe her. Insensitive, strident voice, reasonably intelligent, thinks she's far brighter than she is; believes she is God's special gift to this place, as the expert in all financial matters."

Annie smiled. "Otherwise, I suppose a good and dutiful nun – just hard to live with, I would think. I hazard a guess that Josepha finds her a difficult colleague in the work they do, but I'm equally sure she does the work well and would be scrupulously honest. My time with her was a complete waste; she knows nothing of the robbery, or anything about Sister Josepha at all. I think, apart from work matters, they have no personal conversations at all – other than what courtesy requires."

Mother Benedicta smiled briefly and, nodding abstractedly, changed the subject. She picked up a page from her desk. "Annie,

I've had a strange call from a woman known as Sarah Bellows. She has asked to see me about one of our girls working in Kings Cross."

"Not, Pamela Scott?"

"How did you know that, Annie? What aren't you telling me?"

"No, truly, I know nothing of Sarah Bellows. I just remembered that the delightful young woman, Pamela Scott, spoke of her while I was staying with Monica. We visited the Parkers; Pamela works as a maid for that family."

"Is there any problem with the girl?"

"It's possible there could be. The cook at the Parkers, Peggy Thompson, spoke to me about a young man that Pamela had met. It appears that the cook is worried about the girl and dubious about the man."

"It's always about some man or other, isn't it Annie? Oh well, I'll hear all about it tomorrow. I told Miss Bellows that I'd see her after Vespers tomorrow afternoon."

Mother Benedicta picked up her pen from the desk. "Now, Annie, I'm going to send you packing. I must attend to these government matters – they are fairly urgent. Go and talk to Sister Clare, she's the one who prepares the girls for facing the big, bad world. You'll like Clare; she's a very funny woman and a very good nun."

Benedicta's brow cleared; she smiled, remembering. "I forgot, Annie, you already know her; you covered her in toffee that time you came here pretending to be an expert toffee maker." Both women chuckled quietly at the memory.

39

Saturday night was always a very busy night for the Falcon and his men. He knew the only way to keep on top was to be on his guard continually; also to be *visible* as a constant reminder of who he was – *and* the power he wielded.

Usually at one stage of the night, he walked down the main street of Kings Cross between his two closest henchmen. This often was similar to a Royal progress. Those in the know, moved quickly aside not to impede his path. Any foolish soldier, or pavement idler, who didn't move quickly enough, was promptly and effectively dealt with by Tarzan and Jane.

This Saturday night, he made a personal call on the establishment known as The Crosslands Gentlemen's Club. He was not pleased to be informed, by her second in command, that Sarah was unwell; was 'unable to see him'.

She had left a message to say that she would see him at his house on the following Monday; unfortunately, she did not think she would be well enough before then.

He didn't believe that for a moment, but decided to go along with the deceit: it would throw her off guard. He would be ready for her when she turned up on Monday. He would have his plans for dealing with her 'bloody brat' finished before then.

Saturday nights, besides being very busy – taking reports from all his associates, checking, admonishing, approving – were also very tiring. By two o'clock Sunday mornings the Falcon was ready for bed and, once there, usually was asleep within minutes.

This night followed the regular pattern. Apart from the difficulty regarding Sarah, there were no other major problems, so when the Falcon, yawning widely, was ready for bed, he went to sleep almost immediately.

One floor below, Angelina had been stationed at the open dumb-waiter for hours listening for the return of the men upstairs. She heard them come home, some desultory talking, a final drink and then the preparations for bed.

After she had heard the beginning of the snoring from the main bedroom, she waited another fifteen minutes, glad for once that the irritating snoring was a feature of the Falcon's sleeping pattern – it would cover up any noise she might make with the mechanism of the safe.

She climbed carefully into the dumb-waiter with a large, empty pillow case, drew her knees up to her chin, pulled the rope inside the box-like hole and slowly ascended, hand over hand, to the Falcon's apartment.

The dumbwaiter stopped when it reached the top floor in the Falcon's study. Arriving there, Angelina gently pushed the sliding side of the box open and stepped silently out. She was standing just a few feet from the safe.

Well, she thought, with God's help. I'll do it. Now, the numbers again? She ran through them in her mind, before moving: 57281. Yes, that's right … now … Go ahead…*Do it!*

She advanced quietly to the safe and saying the numbers in her head, successfully managed to open it. Angelina then took from the safe all the money that was stacked neatly in bound bundles, put it into the pillow case, then, carefully searching the safe removed from it what else she thought she might need.

40

Sunday

The Falcon usually slept late on Sunday mornings and it was rare for him to call for breakfast before ten o'clock, or even later. Angelina knew she had to move fast to get to The Junction and back again. She was surprised to hear the movement of the two guards early. They were up and about and had left the house before she was ready to leave. That was unusual. I wonder what they're up to; they'd had a late night, too. It was puzzling.

She crept out of the house with a basket on her arm, just after five o'clock and was able to catch an early tram to Central, then an almost empty train which deposited her at The Junction at a quarter past six o'clock. She hurried in the half light to the Convent gate and rang the bell, keeping her finger on the bell so that it would have to be answered. She noticed the lights on in the Chapel and, with the street door open, could hear the voices of the nuns chanting the Psalms.

Eventually, there was a sound behind the gate door. A voice demanded: "Yes? Who is it?" Angelina replied in a soft voice. "Sister, just open the door a little way. I have something to give you."

When the nun behind the door realised that it was a woman and the voice was not young, the top half of the door began to open. Sister Agatha peered out: "Where are you?"

"Here," replied Angelina, holding up her basket before her face. "Sister, take the basket. Don't take any notice of the potatoes on the top. Look underneath the cloth, you'll find all the money that was stolen." She pushed the basket toward the nun's face and once it had been grasped, ran as fast as she could down the street towards the open door of the Chapel.

Quickly slipping inside the public part of the Chapel, Angelina realised that they were preparing for Mass. That's a lucky break, she thought. I can stay for Mass and then hurry back; I'll still be in time for their breakfasts. She pulled her black shawl up over her head and, kneeling near the grill, scanned the rows of nuns in their stalls, looking for a particular face.

She had difficulty in finding the nun she wanted; with their heads bowed, they all looked alike, but just then a little bell rang and they rose to their feet and, in doing so, one looked towards the grill. Angelina gasped in delight. "My own baby," she cried. "God protect her and keep her safe forever," she prayed fervently – unaware that she had spoken audibly.

Annie, kneeling in the back pew, had noticed the elderly woman with the black shawl and thought she looked familiar. It couldn't be, could it? Annie then heard the woman's exclamation. She looked closely at the nun who had attracted the woman's attention. It had to be Sister Josepha – she was the only one who had turned towards the grill. So that's who Sister Josepha is! She's the daughter of Angelina Falconi!

Stranger and stranger, thought Annie. Why did Sister Josepha – and her mother – have to keep that secret? Should I let her know I've seen her; that I know her? Perhaps not; I'll just wait and see what she does after Mass. I'll catch up with her then.

Annie's proposed plans came to nothing. Angelina, coming back from the grill where she had been looking at her daughter, suddenly caught a glimpse of Annie in the back row. Her face registered shock.

As Annie smiled and went to speak to the older woman, Angelina gave a stifled gasp and fled through the street door.

By the time Annie had reached the street, Angelina had gone. Slowly and thoughtfully, Annie returned to the public Chapel for the Mass.

41

Pamela Scott was running a little late for the early Mass and checking to see that she had her Mass Missal with her and a scarf to cover her head, she slipped out of the kitchen door quietly. Pausing to put the scarf on her head, she was suddenly grabbed by two men.

Terrified, she went to scream, but a pad was slapped across her nose and mouth, and the foul, sickly smell of chloroform permeated her senses.

She struggled frantically, realising she had little time left before she lost consciousness, so used her legs to kick wildly, but soon the struggles subsided, and she slipped downwards in a frightening dark spiral of descent to complete unconsciousness.

Tarzan and Jane picked Pamela up and, holding her between them, went back to the car pretending to talk to the unconscious girl. Reaching the car, they opened the back door, and threw her in. Pamela went sprawling over the back seat. The door was closed, the men got into the front seat, the car started and fifteen minutes later they were carting their unconscious victim into a sleazy, run-down, condemned, filthy, three storey establishment run by a woman who resembled the building she lived in.

Daphne Porter was fifty-four years of age and had a coarse, raddled face. The long horse-like mane of hair, dyed an aggressive yellow, did nothing to hide the age of the old prostitute. A cigarette was hanging from the corner of her mouth; her rheumy eyes were already assuming the appearance of old age, dissipation and disease.

Daphne looked, without interest, as the two men brought in the new girl. She had seen hundreds of new girls arrive. Once it had aroused her pity, now she watched with complete indifference. She was far more interested in a glass of Bacardi rum 151 which she held reverently in her hand.

It was the first time she had ever savoured the fiery liquid. A drunken American sailor had given her two whole bottles which he had stolen from the officers' mess.

Daphne was amazed, thrilled, at the startling effects of the rum. She had placed the bottles with great care, on the little desk in her office. She drank the golden liquor, with tiny appreciative sips, as she mindlessly surveyed the scene taking place in front of her.

When spoken to brusquely by the two men, Daphne pulled herself together, and led the men to the room she had chosen for the new girl. She stepped back as they threw Pamela onto the bed. The men left, locking the door after them. Handing the key back to Daphne, they reminded the woman of the strict instructions from the Falcon regarding the girl.

A couple of girls, who had nearly finished working for the night, walked past with their men while this was happening; they gazed with weary disinterest at the familiar scene. One girl, however, slowed her pace a little as she actually recognized the unconscious girl. She hesitated, perplexed, her drugged, dull eyes troubled.

Suddenly shrugging her shoulders, Maureen told herself it was not her job to help in any way, but still uneasily troubled, hurried after the man who was calling her impatiently.

She desperately needed three things: to get this one over, get another fix quickly, then lose herself in the blessed relief of sleep.

42

Angelina, as soon as she returned to the house, took an apron and rushed to the stove to begin cooking the meal. As she was finishing the preparations for breakfast, the buzzer sounded. They were ready up-stairs.

She took the large tray set for three people and placed it in the dumb-waiter. She had no idea whether the two body-guards had returned or not, but it would not be expected that she *would* know, so she had wisely prepared the meal for three people. It was fortunate she had done so, as she heard the three of them talking as they began to eat.

The tired woman would have returned to her work, but her ears tuned into the subject of their conversation. Merciful God in Heaven! They were now talking about that young child Lucky had brought to see her! Almighty God, will it ever end?

The exhausted woman held her head in her hands. Am I never to have any peace? But what about the child? There's no hope for her; she's an innocent baby – another one – and now *they've actually kidnapped her!* What in God's name have they already done to her?

Angelina sat down on the floor near the opening to the dumb-waiter, her head against the wall. She closed her eyes: how can you do this to me? I've tried so hard. You cannot ask more of me, she pleaded.

A sudden terrifying solution occurred to her …No, she almost screamed in horror! Not *that*! … Especially, that! … Please God … No! I can't! . .. You can't ask me to do *that*!

43

Paolo Falconi began to put the second part of his plan into action. He picked up the phone and dialled quickly. "Sarah, this is the Falcon. Don't talk, just listen. I thought you might just like to know that the little girl, Pamela Scott, has been taken from her friends' house and is well hidden. You won't see her again or, if you do, you will not recognize her, will you? Not after she's been on the game for a few weeks. Just thought you'd like to know."

The Falcon laughed. "It's just like old times, isn't it? You thought you didn't have a daughter, and now, once again, you have no daughter – everything's back to normal. I like that!" The Falcon laughed loudly and replaced the receiver.

Sarah stood with the receiver in her hand in a state of shock. She could hardly believe what she had just heard. It had never crossed her mind that the Falcon would act so swiftly; so viciously. Gradually, as the shock began to wear off, Sarah slowly replaced the receiver, stared into space and began automatically to tidy her office. What, in God's name, could she do, she wondered? I have to find out where Pamela is! How can I do that?

As her fingers performed the ordinary tasks, an idea came into her head. What about the girls in her own house? They were all professionals, but, on the whole, given their work, they were decent enough girls.

They would be as angry as I am, at some innocent girl being

abducted. I think I could trust them to keep the enquiries quiet. It's worth a try anyhow; I must do something; this might be the last chance I'll be given in my whole life. Her eyes closed in terror as she thought of what they might already have done to her child.

Please, *please God*, she prayed, *no cocaine*, I beg of you, no cocaine! Don't let them make her an addict – she'd be lost then; there's no coming back from that!

44

As the Mass in the Convent Chapel finished, Annie was aware that someone was hissing at her from the other side of the grill. She turned around, surprised, to see the wrinkled face of Sister Agatha beckoning to her urgently. Annie hurried to the grill and the old nun whispered: "The money's back, Miss Anne. It was all handed in before Mass in an old shopping basket covered with potatoes. I kept it beside me during the Mass, and now I've given it to Mother. She's going to tell the community about it now in Chapter."

"Did you see who handed it in, Sister," Annie asked.

"Not really. However, it was not a young voice that spoke to me; it was an older woman's voice. When I managed to get the gate open, with all the locks, I peered down the street and caught a glimpse of a woman in black clothes running. I wouldn't be able to recognize her again." Sister Agatha paused, and turned her head away from Annie. "Oh, excuse me Miss Anne, Mother wants to talk to you."

"Open the grill door, Sister Agatha, I want Annie to come inside now," Benedicta ordered. A door in the grill was quickly unlocked. Annie expressed her surprise; she didn't know there was a part of the grill that opened to a full door. "Necessary for the cleaning and for opening and closing the street door," explained the Superior absently.

"Annie, come and see the basket of money; I've never seen anything so fantastic in my whole life. I thought you would like to see it before I take it to the Chapter meeting." Annie followed her Aunt through the Chapel and out to the sacristy where Sister Michael was standing guarding a basket of what looked like potatoes.

"This is curious affair, and no mistake, Aunt," Annie observed. "Who ever heard of bringing money back disguised as a basket of vegetables? However, it was a pretty clever thing to do if you are carrying such a huge amount of money in public today."

Annie quickly lifted some potatoes and counted the bundles of money. "I don't know if I'm wrong or not, Aunt, but I think there's far more here than the two thousand pounds; it looks closer to three, I think."

Both nuns were surprised; Annie suggested that they put the wretched money quickly into the safe in the Superior's office. They didn't want any more disappearing tricks.

Before she left her aunt, Annie whispered to her that she had discovered Sister Josepha's surname: it was *Falconi* and her mother was still alive. She had been at Mass in the public Chapel, but when she recognized Annie, she had fled.

Mother Benedicta stood still in shock, her eyes wide with astonishment, then recovering quickly, said she would notify the Mother House and ask for all the information she could get about the nun. She then excused herself; she had to go to the Chapter meeting.

Annie, suddenly at a loose end, and not knowing exactly what to do with herself, before breakfast, decided to visit the older girls in their section of the institution – the ones who were ready to leave the shelter of the Home. She was always welcome there and she knew most of them by name. Walking across the playground, Annie suddenly felt oppressed; her steps slowed and she was uneasy.

Something was frighteningly wrong somewhere. It hasn't ended with the return of the money, she decided – there is still more evil to come.

Annie shrugged her shoulders as if she would shake off this weird feeling of impending disaster; of being helpless at being able to prevent it – *whatever 'it'* was. She pulled herself together; it was not like her to be morbid or fanciful.

Just then she heard the chatter of the senior girls and their giggling; that was just what she needed to chase away the black thoughts … her strange fears. She composed her face, smoothing out the worry lines and made her way to the girls' common room from which she could hear the laughter.

Yes, this is exactly what I need, she decided, nodding her head in satisfaction.

45

As the time was approaching nine o'clock, Annie was in the midst of having her hair done by one of the girls who wanted someone, with long hair, to practise on.

Using a magazine as a guide, Rosie, the aspiring hairdresser, operating in an admiring circle of girls, was attempting to do a complicated arrangement and had almost succeeded, when Annie's rebellious hair tumbled down, to the delight of the observers.

They had all collapsed in laughter, Rosie and Annie included. Mother Benedicta appeared suddenly in the doorway. The girls respectfully stood up. Benedicta greeted them and spoke to her niece keeping her voice even and casual, while forcing herself to smile at the girls.

"Annie, you look even more wild-looking than usual with that hairdo. Rosie, we'll have to get Mrs Watson back here for you to practise on – by the look of it, more practice is needed.

"I'm sorry, Annie, to drag you away, but would you come with me now please, something has turned up." Annie took one look at her Aunt's face and hurriedly waved to the girls, followed the Superior to her office trying desperately to put her long hair into some semblance of order.

As soon as they were inside the door, Mother Benedicta began to speak, her face crumpled, lined with emotion and worry. "Annie, I've just had a phone call from a Mr Parker where Pamela Scott works as a maid. She's …"

"Quickly, Mother, just continue. I know the girl. What's happened?"

"I've just received information that Pamela Scott was violently abducted this morning as she was setting out for the early Mass at Darlinghurst. Chloroform was used, they think. Inspector Henderson at Kings Cross has been notified; they are searching for the girl already, but she could be anywhere."

Annie was as shocked as her aunt. "Dear God! Mrs Thomson, the cook there, was worried about that young man Pamela had met, remember? And the whole King Cross area is a den of vice – she could be taken anywhere … No, that's not right – not just anywhere; this has been done for some definite reason or other." Annie made a decision.

"Aunt, I'll just grab my hat and purse and I'm off. I'll go first to the Parker house and speak to the cook. You tell the Sisters to pray for this child and don't forget to find out all you can about Sister Josepha … *Wait* a minute! Wait a minute!"

Annie closed her eyes tight. "*Her* surname is Falconi! Angelina Falconi was in the Chapel this morning and called Sister Josepha her child! The young man that Pamela Scott had met – the one the cook was worried about – *his* name was Falconi as well! Dear God what is going on with that family? We're caught in some nightmare *connected with that family*.

"When Angelina Falconi was here this morning, she brought back the money – I'll bet my life, that's what she was doing! It's all beginning to tie up – it's all connected in some way."

Annie kissed her aunt quickly and ran from the room. Within fifteen minutes, she was sitting in a fast train which was carrying her swiftly to the city.

46

It had been utter confusion in the Parker's household. When Mrs Thomson had come down to the kitchen to begin the preparations for breakfast, she expected to see Pamela working there. She'd been surprised to find no one there, but shrugged, thinking that the young woman must have been kept longer at Church – perhaps it had been a long sermon, she vaguely surmised. She began to get the things ready herself.

As the clock moved on, Pamela still had not returned. Peggy Thomson was filled with a vague sense of foreboding. She actually went out the kitchen door, thinking she would have a quick look up the road to see if she could see the young girl on her way back.

She stopped in her tracks just outside the door. Pamela's Mass book – a beautiful gift of which she had been very proud – was lying on the paving stones, the back split open and holy cards scattered everywhere. Peggy stared in horror, as next to the Mass book, was the scarf that Pamela always wore to Church.

Thoroughly alarmed now, Peggy had hurried upstairs, glad to find that Tom Parker was up and about. He saw her and bade her Good Morning.

"It's a lovely late summer morning Mrs Thomson," he had begun when he noticed her troubled face. "Is anything the matter? Has something happened?"

"Mr Parker, I think Pamela – the new maid – has been attacked and I think, abducted."

The elderly man had risen to his feet. "What! Are you sure? How can you tell?"

Peggy burst into tears. "Come and see, sir, I think it happened just as she left for Church this morning. She goes to the early Mass, but she's always back in time to help me with the breakfast. Now …" Peggy held her apron up to her eyes. "Oh, what have they done to her?"

"Good God! Let me see what you've seen? Then I'll ring the police. I know Inspector Henderson well." Tom Parker had hurried with Peggy to the kitchen, through the door and took in the scene of the struggle. "Wait a minute, Mrs Thomson." He sniffed the air delicately. "Am I mistaken or is that a faint odour of chloroform, or am I imagining things?"

Peggy blew her nose then sniffed carefully. There was definitely a trace of that awful smell. When she realised what she had smelt, Peggy burst out crying again. "Oh my God! The fiends! What have they done to the child?" She turned to her employer.

"For the love of God, Mr Parker, ring the police. There's not a moment to lose if they are ever to find her in this area." Tom Parker patting the cook's shoulders, greatly disturbed, hurried upstairs to the phone.

47

It was still only ten o'clock when Annie arrived at the Parker's house. She was greeted by a worried husband and wife who briefly explained what appeared to have happened to the girl Pamela. At Annie's urgent request, they led her to Peggy Thomson in the kitchen, where they left her alone with the cook.

Mrs Thomson insisted on making a fresh cup of tea when she discovered that Annie had not bothered with breakfast after Mass. She hurried about the kitchen and soon had tea and toast before Annie and, at Annie's urging, had another cup of tea herself.

"Mrs Watson," Peggy began, but Annie cut her short.

"Please, call me Annie – everyone calls me that. This is far too important for any standing on formality. Peggy, just tell me the events of this morning as you have told the police."

Peggy went through the explanation again and then showed Annie the Mass book still lying where it had fallen with the scattered holy cards. The cook said: "These can be gathered up now; the police said they would only have Pamela's prints on them anyhow." Annie started to pick up the cards and place them inside the cover of the damaged book.

Her heart constricted as she noticed that so many of the cards were from the Sisters, or from girls of her group, from the Home. Taking the book and scarf inside the house she asked Peggy to keep the book safe as it was precious to Pamela. They sat down at the table again.

"Tell me, Peggy, when Pamela was telling you all about her boy friend, and the day out she had in his company, did she mention where she had been in detail?"

"She did, indeed, Annie," the cook screwed up her eyes in thought. "Yes, first she told me the boy friend, Lucky, took her to meet his mother ..."

"His mother? Quickly, Peggy, did she tell you where the mother lived?"

"Not in detail. She did say it was not far to walk from the top of the Cross. And she also said that it was a beautiful, very large and very tall house. I think that would mean that it was an old Victorian terrace – they are very grand in this area."

"Good. You are a very good witness. Did Pamela talk about the mother? You see I have met the woman, believe it or not, at Monica Jeffrey's place. What did Pamela think of her? What was she like? Did she say anything definite about her?"

"Again, I can say she did. Mrs Falconi – that's the mother's name – is Italian, she was dressed completely in black, including a black shawl, with a black scarf over her grey hair and lives in a house filled with religious pictures and a large crucifix."

"Was Pamela made welcome by the mother?"

"She told me a strange thing, Annie. She said that the mother appeared terrified and was so overcome at the little gift of lavender that Pamela had taken her, that she had hugged the young girl and cried."

"Did the visit last long?"

"No, the mother was so strange that Pamela suggested to Lucky that she seemed to be only disturbing the woman so they should leave, which they did."

"Where did they go then?"

"To some place called The Crosslands Gentlemen's Club, run by a woman called Sarah – they had morning tea there."

"I wonder what that means. A Gentlemen's *Club*?" Annie murmured, uneasily. "I suppose it could be a restaurant, or … please God, not a …"

"What? Annie, you're frightening me," cried Peggy.

"I was thinking that it could be a high class brothel. It does sound far-fetched, but with the manner of Pamela's abduction, it would fit in."

Peggy began to cry again. "Oh, God in Heaven, I hope you're wrong."

Annie held the cook's hand. "Believe me, Peggy, so do I." She stood up. "Anyhow, I'm going to find out, first from the police, where Mrs Falconi lives, and then I'm going to find this Sarah woman … wait a minute, wait a minute … Mother Benedicta said something to me about a woman called 'Sarah', Peggy….Was the surname 'Bellows', by any chance?"

Peggy's eyes opened wide with surprise. "I do believe it was the name. Yes, Sarah Bellows at the Gentlemen's Club, that's what Pamela said."

"Then all is not lost. That woman is coming to see Mother Benedicta this afternoon. I think there's a connection between Pamela and that woman – unknown to the girl." Annie gave the cook a quick hug. "I'll go out the kitchen door, Peggy, save time. I'm going to find out where those women live, or give it a damn good try, anyhow." Annie slipped out the kitchen door and was soon walking quickly towards the Cross.

48

Pamela awoke with a terrible headache and nausea – she had a very strong sensation of wanting to vomit. She had started to rise from this strange bed she had found herself in, when a wave of dizziness and nausea overcame her; she fell back on the thin pillow.

Where on earth am I, she wondered. What am I doing here? I don't live here. Have I gone back to the Home? No, my room was never like this – this is *awful*.

Pamela looked around the room, careful to move her head slowly. She gazed at the horrible wall paper – ghastly big red roses, the paper peeling from the walls, an iron bedstead with dirty linen, a kitchen chair; a framed print of a little girl cuddling a kitten, faded and fly-spotted.

It was a terrible room and she was sure she had never, ever been in this place before. How on earth did she ever get here?

With a heart stopping jolt, she suddenly remembered starting off for Mass this morning – or, *was* it this morning? There were two men; she remembered being grabbed and also being aware that her precious Mass book had fallen.

Tears filled her eyes when she thought of that book. It was Mother Benedicta's gift to her, when she had managed to get this position – it had cost a lot of money, she knew that, and Mother had written in the fly leaf: 'To our beloved daughter, Pamela.'

Slowly, and with great difficulty, Pamela began to realise she had been abducted. With that awareness, she knew she had to try to get out of this place – wherever this place was!

Slowly she rose from the bed, held briefly onto the iron bars at the foot of the bed and stood up.

The world was spinning dangerously, but by standing perfectly still, Pamela managed to control the vertigo. She moved very slowly to the door and softly turned the handle. It was locked securely. She went to the window and found that she could see the tops of other buildings so realised that she was on the second, or even the third floor. No escape that way either. She stood still and listened intently.

There were sounds from outside the door, people moving about. Would it be safe to call out? Perhaps safer to just stay put until she felt better; then to try to bang on the door.

Very soon she realised she could stand no longer, and groping her way with difficulty, back to the filthy bed, was just glad to be able to lie down once again.

49

A car pulled into the kerb just in front of Annie as she was hurrying along the street and she was startled to hear her own name being called. She looked at the car and saw, to her surprise, Peggy Thomson, the cook whom she had left at the Parker's house only fifteen minutes before.

"Mrs Watson, Mrs Watson, please come here," Peggy called, with her head out the window. When Annie had hurried across to the car, Peggy told her to get into the back seat. Only then did Annie notice the young man at the wheel. That must be the Parker's son, John, she realised. He spoke first.

"Mrs Watson, I'm John Parker. Peggy has told me about the situation; that you are desperately anxious to find out about Sarah Bellow's Club, as well as the Falconi house. I happen to know both. Thank the good Lord, I'm staying at my parents' place this weekend. I was still in bed when you were there, but dad came and told me about this abominable crime."

"Thank God for that, John," Annie replied. "I was wondering how on earth I was going to find those places, but I was going to try; anything to save that poor child."

"Well, Peggy told me you dreaded that the Gentlemen's Club where Sarah Bellows works might be a brothel. Well, I'm afraid you're right. It *is* a brothel but a very high class one – ultra respectable, with a very important clientele." He gave a little rueful laugh.

"Well known, I'm sorry to say, to the eminent legal profession. However, it's not very far now. I'll wait outside with Peggy, while you go inside. If you need any help just shout and we'll come barging in, but I think you might do better on your own with Sarah."

Annie was wise enough not to ask just how the young barrister knew the place so intimately – and the Madame as well. Instead, she thanked them both for their help. Very soon they pulled up alongside a three storey building which looked like one of the better kind of old fashioned hotels; one where you still managed to get real service.

There was nothing flashy, or garish, about the place and the couple of young women entering could have been top secretaries in important business offices. Annie realised that they were nothing of the kind.

Climbing out of the car, Annie approached the main doorway, then entering, found herself in a beautifully decorated vestibule, with a receptionist desk and a bell on it, with instructions to ring if attention was required.

After ringing the bell, Annie was surprised to see a flustered young woman hurry from an inside office. The young woman who looked worried, made an effort to be professional but, clearly, had no idea what she was supposed to say or do.

"You are the manageress?" Annie asked coldly in her beautiful, cultured voice.

"Well, yes, in a manner of speaking, I am … that is, I mean …"

"Either you are, or you are not," Annie declared in a voice that brooked no nonsense. "*Are* you?" The girl appeared uncertain how to answer this question.

"Well, not really, you see, Madame Sarah asked me to look after the desk for a while … she is not well."

"Tell her, immediately, that I am the daughter of Lady Mary Sheridan and I demand to speak to her. I have come from the Lady Benedicta. She may prefer speaking to me, rather than to the police."

"The police!"

"Exactly. Don't waste my time, girl. Take me to her at once," Annie ordered. The girl looked uncertain, glancing back into the inner room. She then, nervously, beckoned this imperious – and obviously important – woman to follow her. Annie followed the girl into another room. She stopped dead … her eyes staring in disbelief.

Annie had very nearly gasped aloud when she saw the woman sitting behind a desk. The woman had hair still golden, a tragic face and to Annie's complete stupefaction, she found herself looking at an older image of the missing girl, Pamela Scott.

The two women, one so young and this one about forty years of age, were so alike, that Annie felt weak; she quickly had to sit down, uninvited. It had never occurred to Annie that Pamela's mother could still be living, but the similarity was so outstanding, so bewilderingly alike, this woman could be nothing else!

Never had Annie dreamt of this – it was the stuff of nightmares; all her autocratic front collapsed, in her shock.

Deflated, Annie was unsure how to proceed; what was the right way, now, to approach this whole affair? With the disappearance of the imperious, demanding persona she had adopted, Annie now appeared to be what she actually was: an ordinary woman facing an extraordinary situation, the like of which she had never before experienced.

She stared at the woman in stunned silence, her eyes big and her mouth slightly open. She swallowed several times trying desperately to find her voice.

50

Mother Benedicta was never patient for long when making long distance telephone calls. She was totally convinced that most of the operators chose only the most inconvenient times to interrupt. This time she actually snapped angrily, as she declared: "Yes, of course I want another three minutes; there's no need for all that ridiculous 'Go ahead please, nonsense' I intend to go ahead if you'd only keep out of the conversation."

The telephonist was unperturbed. "Go ahead please." Benedicta gritted her teeth in exasperation, and proceeded with her call.

"Mother General," Mother Benedicta explained once again, "I would never dream of asking for these personal details if the situation were not urgent."

The voice of the aged nun spoke calmly. "Mother Benedicta, just tell me the whole story, slowly and carefully. This is a very special and unusual case and I'll have to get advice from the Bishop before I can proceed..."

"From the Bishop? Whatever for?"

"Please, Mother, that is not for you to know ... yet. Tell me what the trouble is concerning Sister Mary Josepha, then why it is so necessary to reveal to you the details you say you need."

"But there is no time for all this ..."

"You said there was a robbery," the General went on serenely.

"Yes, but that has turned out to be a 'non-robbery'; the money was returned. Sister Josepha appears definitely involved, but not of her own free will ..."

"Explain."

"Look Mother, I don't have time..."

The operator's voice broke in. "Three minutes is up. Do you wish to continue?"

"Oh course I do, you silly woman," shouted Benedicta. "Get off the phone!"

The Mother General reprimanded Benedicta for her rudeness and demanded that she do as she was told – tell her the whole story.

"There's a nun's freedom at stake here; she could be sent to goal," angrily explained Benedicta, through clenched teeth. "Surely that should be sufficient reason enough for you to do as I ask. I simply don't have time to waste on ..."

There was a hint of amusement in the reply. "Well, if you will only do as you are requested, Mother, the time will be shortened greatly. So, control your impatience and start at the beginning." The voice sharpened. '*That*, Mother, is an order."

Benedicta realising that she had no option, biting her lips in vexation, began with the story of the robbery ... only to be interrupted again by that detested impersonal voice: "Three minutes is up; do you wish to continue?"

Benedicta bit back the reply she wanted to make, and hissed, "Yes." She then continued ..."and we have already discovered that Sister Josepha's real name is Falconi and that's the name of a notorious gangster in Sydney ..."

Benedicta, clutching her long rosary beads in frustration with her left hand, continued with the full story – forcing her voice to remain calm.

51

In the Crosslands Gentlemen's Club office, Annie finally found she could speak:

"You are Pamela's mother," she stated. The golden-haired woman trembled. She raised a tear-stricken face and spoke hesitantly, "I think … I must be."

"You didn't know?" Annie asked in wonder. "But, you have seen her; she's the living image of you."

"I know," Sarah replied. "I have been in a mental fog ever since the monster's grandson brought her here to visit me the other day. I couldn't believe my eyes – it was like looking into a mirror and …" The woman began to cry helplessly. "He'd told me the baby had died six weeks after he'd left her at the Orphanage, all those years ago."

Annie moved her chair closer and took the weeping woman's hand. "Look, I'm Annie Watson, Mother Benedicta is my aunt – she's the Superior at that Orphanage. I was there this morning when we got the news that Pamela had been abducted. I know you were going to see Mother this afternoon. Are you aware that Pamela had been abducted?"

Sarah looked at Annie in anguish. "Yes," she whispered. "The Falcon phoned me with the shocking news. I don't know where she is; I have asked the girls here to be on the lookout for her. They are basically decent girls, and, I believe, are fond of me, so they will try their hardest to find her for me." Sarah's voice changed.

"Mrs Watson, if we do not find her I'm terrified for her." Sarah abandoned her self-restraint and wept without restraint. Annie held the distraught woman, but realised that there was no time to be lost. She deliberately pushed on with the questioning.

"Were you coming to see Mother Benedicta about the possibility of Pamela being your child?"

"Yes, I was," the other answered. "Mrs Watson, before God, I had no idea Pamela had lived. At the time I had no way of caring for the child, I was penniless and deserted.

"A gangster came to me offering assistance; he arranged for the baby girl to be taken to the Orphanage and then informed me that my child had died, as I told you. I had then to repay him for his assistance."

Sarah raised a tear-streaked face. "Mrs Watson, I gladly worked for that man in gratitude, as I had no one else to help me and have worked for him running this … this place … ever since. All these years and he had lied to me! He had betrayed the most precious and innocent thing I had ever done in my life."

"You saw your child on Friday didn't you?"

The woman was surprised, "Yes, that's when it was. I rang the owner of this Club immediately Lucky and Pamela had left here."

"Did you, by any chance, abuse him? Tell him how he had betrayed you? That you, perhaps, were not working for him anymore?" Sarah's eyes opened wide in astonishment.

"That is exactly what I did do." Sarah paused. "Oh my God! That is the reason for the abduction of Pamela! He was making it clear to me that no one gets away with thwarting him." She burst out crying again. "But where would he take her? Dear God, by now, he might have given her cocaine."

Annie looked startled. "Cocaine? Yes … I suppose he's involved in that, too, if he controls brothels." She now spoke sharply to Sarah.

'Sarah, stop! Weeping will get us nowhere. Now, you would know the places the gangster actually owns, or where he could call in favours. Come with me and we will search each and every one."

Annie paused, as she thought of something else. "Sarah, could you throw a few things in a case – you cannot come back here; you could stay with my Aunt at the Home. But get up quickly; we have no time to lose if we are to find your child."

Annie added a practical suggestion: "Sarah, while you're getting a few clothes, you must have the keys of the safe, throw in some money that's lying around as well. You've earned your wages and you have to live." Sarah looked startled at the suggestion, but promised that she would do as Annie said, and hurried from the room.

Annie ran outside to the waiting car, told Peggy Thomson and John Parker what had happened and that she would be bringing out some luggage in a moment. They looked astonished, but nodded acceptance. Annie returned to the office.

She found Sarah with the young girl from the front vestibule there. On the desk in front of an open safe was a huge pile of money. She stood and listened as Sarah hurriedly listed the things she wanted done.

"Count the money, carefully, Debbie. Divide it into twenty equal amounts and make sure that each girl gets the same. He'll not get one penny of this lot. Tell them I have left; the place will be raided soon by the police and to get out as quickly as they can. Tell them I am very sorry and," her voice broke, "give them my love." She picked up a small suitcase and followed Annie to the car.

John jumped out and took the case from Sarah. He offered to drive the two women wherever they wanted, but Annie refused. She explained that she and Sarah would go alone but, if they could, they would come back to his parents' house when their search was over. Annie remembered the luggage they had stacked in the boot and asked John if he would take it back to his home, she would be grateful – they'd collect it later.

Peggy declared that, no matter what time that would be, there would be a meal waiting for them.

Annie spoke quietly to John before they drove away. "Ring, Inspector Henderson, John, tell him what we've found out, but give the girls time to get out of Sarah's place before they raid it – it's only fair to the poor girls." He nodded his understanding and drove away. Soon after, Annie and Sarah began their search.

"I think, Mrs Watson," Sarah advised, "we'll start at the nearest brothel and work from there. I think the Falcon would have chosen one of these for Pamela. The supervisors would be afraid to tell anyone about it and the girls likewise."

"Let's hurry, Sarah and for the love of Mike call me Annie. And, now – while we're walking – you can tell me why your name is Bellows while Pamela's is Scott and, also where does Lucky live, for we're going visiting there as well."

52

By half past one o'clock both Annie and Sarah were foot-sore and exhausted. They had visited several brothels and while Sarah had spoken to the working girls, Annie had interrogated the supervisor using every aspect of her powerful personality to intimidate the individual, in order to get at the truth. But it had all been to no avail. There was no trace of the missing girl.

Both women were keenly aware that the longer it was before Pamela was found, the more dangerous it was for her. They had had an interview with Inspector Henderson. The police, too, had been unable to trace the girl. The inspector had also informed them that he had raided Sarah's place but, strange to note, by the time they got there, no girls were to be found. The place was deserted.

Both tired women kept their faces expressionless.

By two o'clock, Annie made a decision. She hailed a taxi, and they were driven to the Parker's house. Annie had to phone Mother Benedicta and they desperately needed to have something to eat and drink.

Peggy was still waiting for them and, within a few minutes, placed food before the women, as she had promised she would. John came down to the kitchen and listened as they told of their fruitless search. After eating and drinking two cups of tea, Annie asked if she could use their phone upstairs, as she must contact Mother Benedicta, who would be beside herself with worry. There was also another matter that was urgent. John led the way to the phone and left Annie to make the call.

When Annie asked to speak to Mother Benedicta, this time there was no delay. The Superior was waiting for the call and quickly responded when called. Annie gave her the disappointing news about Pamela, but insisted that she had not given up, nor had the girl's *mother*.

Annie was aware of the shock that that would be, so waited patiently until Benedicta had expressed her astonishment at this surprise. Annie explained how it had happened, and what had become of the mother, Sarah Bellows, besides the reason for the differences in the names.

With that subject exhausted, Annie asked about the news regarding Sister Josepha from Bathurst. The result was surprising.

"You won't believe this, Annie, but the name on her file is 'Sister Mary Josepha, formerly Anna *Smith*."

"Smith? You have to be joking. She's Italian and whoever heard of an Italian named Smith?"

"Just hold on, my girl, there's more to come," Benedicta cautioned. "Her file has a sealed brown envelope inside the actual file. On the outside of the file is written: "Sister's name has been changed from her true surname in order to protect her. Inside the envelope are her original certificates of Baptism, Holy Communion, and Confirmation plus the necessary references. This envelope and the certificates, are not to be opened until death – or a similar urgent necessity, would require them." The seal is that of the previous Mother General of the Order and – listen to this, Annie – the Bishop of the Diocese, who is now dead."

"How extraordinary!" Annie exclaimed. "I've never heard of such a thing."

"I actually have, Annie, once before. It was a case of a nun persecuted, and in such grave danger, that the bishop thought the only way to safeguard her was to do as has been done with Josepha."

"Well, Aunt, at least it shows that we're on the right track. There has to be something wrong, to have taken all that trouble – and convinced your Mother General and the Bishop, that it was necessary. It would appear – if she is, as it seems, involved in the robbery; which of course, is now no robbery – then whoever the person was that she was in danger from, has now found out *where* she is."

"Exactly my thought, too, Annie," agreed the Superior. "However, Mother General is taking advice of the current Bishop this afternoon. He has promised that if he thinks the situation is as serious as it sounds and gives his permission, she will open the sealed envelope and phone me, with the contents of the inner envelope."

"Even though we now know Sister's surname, the documents might still be useful in the details, Aunt. They might shed more light on the mystery, but I think we know everything now about the poor nun. We know her true name; we know her mother is still living, we know she is connected in some way to a gangster named Falconi. There doesn't seem much more that would actually help us," Annie concluded.

"Look, darling, I've still got to get to the house where Pamela's boyfriend lived – he's the grandson apparently of the big-time gangster – and we still must find Pamela, so I'm off. If anything happens, I'll try to get news to you. If all goes well, I'll try to be back by Vespers this afternoon. Bye dear."

Annie was aware that John was signalling to her frantically. She hurried to him. John leant closer to her and whispered. "Peggy's daughter has just come – she's a prostitute and a drug addict, who has broken Peggy's heart. Maureen is her name. She has just told her mother that she saw Pamela being taken into a place called Daphne's. I thought I'd catch you, before you saw the poor wretched creature. They're in the kitchen now."

Annie ran down to the kitchen and found the thin, scantily clad young woman crying on Peggy's ample breast. Sarah was standing away over near the corner of the room, in order to give the cook some privacy.

Peggy turned as Annie entered. "Annie," she said brokenly, "this is my little girl, Maureen."

Maureen turned her eyes to Annie who was shocked to see the pin-points of the pupils and the wide staring blankness of the eyes. She moved towards the girl swiftly, took her from Peggy and put her arms around her. Annie spoke softly.

"Maureen is a beautiful Irish name, do you know that? I'm mostly Irish, and many of my family have that name." The girl looked at this stranger with huge wondering eyes.

"You don't despise me." she whispered, trembling.

"Why should I? You're a lovely girl and your mother's a wonderful woman. And, I think you have come here to help us. If you do, then God will undoubtedly bless you and help you and I can assure you, *we* will, if there is any way you think we can."

The girl started to cry. "I was afraid for her; I didn't want her to end up like me. I heard about her with *his* grandson and I was afraid. If they started her on the game and then fed her on dope she was finished. I didn't know what to do when I saw Tarzan and Jane carry her in this morning." Annie blinked at the extraordinary names.

"So, Pamela is still at Daphne's place is she?" Annie asked calmly, knowing that she must be very careful, otherwise she would frighten this poor girl, but she did wonder who the hell belonged to those two weird names. "Locked in, I suppose. Do you happen to know which room?"

"It's room 47 on the first floor. I asked if I could get her a glass of water but Daphne slapped my face; told me to get back on the street – and earn some money," the tears started to fall again down the raddled face.

"Slapped your face, did she? Well, she's in for a surprise; I'll remember that. Thank you my darling girl," and to the girl's aston-ishment, Annie leant down and kissed her.

With instructions to Peggy to keep Maureen there, even if they had to lock her up, Annie informed the startled mother that, as soon as the Pamela affair was concluded, she would contact Mrs Jeffrey about their cousin, the very famous Doctor Gascoigne-Ridley.

She would get Monica to plead with their cousin, to suggest a place for Maureen in his clinic for treatment. It could be her last chance.

Sarah and Annie then ran out of the kitchen to the car where John was waiting. It was fortunate that Sarah knew where Daphne's place was located. She filled them with forebodings when she told them that it was the sleaziest and filthiest of all the brothels owned by the Falcon and was run by a harridan – actually named Daphne.

53

In the bedroom of his basement apartment, studying his wardrobe, Lucky Falconi made a sudden decision. Yes, a dreary office clerk nothing flashy; that'll be the ticket. He took from the wardrobe a sombre grey suit.

He dressed carefully choosing a conservative white shirt and a grey tie. He combed his hair with the parting on one side then with great reluctance and grimacing, shaved off his 'Fred Astaire' moustache.

He took a pair of plain glass spectacles with steel frames from a drawer, and then looked at himself in the mirror. He laughed. No one would ever recognize him, in this outfit. He was ready. As he headed for the back garage, he carefully checked the gun he carried in his inside coat pocket, then felt for the extra bullets in the side pocket.

As Lucky climbed into the little grey van, he smiled to himself. The Grey Man in his little grey van is about to cause havoc. He laughed happily. "I'm off to Vespers!" he sang out loud then added to himself: This will be a new version of vespers for the black crows! It'll be evening for one of them at least!

54

John Parker came in with the two women as they reached Daphne's place. The building looked as if it were due for demolition: it was in a state of near total and dangerous disrepair.

Annie had discovered, to her surprise, the place was not in the main strip of the Cross, but down near the docks at Woolloomooloo. She shuddered as she stepped into the building. The very rotting appearance of the place; the stench of unwashed bodies nearly over-whelmed her. She was suddenly very glad that John was with them.

There was a door labelled 'Supervisor' as you entered the little hall. Annie rapped smartly on the door. After a couple of moments it was opened by a woman over fifty, with long, dyed, vivid yellow hair, tied back in a ribbon; a thin, raddled face with a huge bosom and wearing a skimpy black skirt. Around her shoulders she wore a bright pink, gauzy, thin stole. She was clutching her blouse with one hand, fumbling to hold it closed while a glass of rum, was waving in the other.

She stared at the two women confronting her. After one look, she started to laugh jeeringly.

"So the bloody aristocracy has condescended to call on the peasantry have they? What the hell do you want? Get out of my place, or I'll get my friend here to throw you out."

She leaned forward and leered at Annie and Sarah. "Or, are you applying for a job here? I'm sorry, but you're both too old and you'd be no bloody good at it, anyhow."

A drunken, slurred, American voice interrupted the tirade. "Nauw, nauw, Daff; we're reg'lar guys 'ere. Bring your sfriends in for … 'lil drink. They wouldn't hever had slhuch drink as schis … as this," there was a loud belch ...'cuse me ... "it's the schrink of d' frogs … gods." So saying, an overweight, American sailor lurched into view behind Daphne at the door.

Daphne was outraged at the suggestion she share the grog. "These bloody tarts aren't getting any of this," she waved her glass around and picked up the bottle with her other hand. "This," she informed Annie and Sarah, solemnly, "sets you on fire. In fact," she started to giggle "It actually *is* flammable!"

Annie was not renowned for her patience, or for her meekness. She had a very strong right arm from her work in the orchard and farm. Without a word being said, she swung back her hand and slapped the woman across the face, sending the glass and the bottle crashing to the floor; Bacardi Rum spilling everywhere, the woman went hurtling backwards until she reached the opposite wall.

"That's for Maureen," Annie announced calmly. Seeing his girl friend in trouble, the drunken sailor staggered belligerently towards the women, his fists clenched.

John reached into the room and with one swift movement, grabbed the sailor by the collar, dragged him out of the room through the front door and threw him in the gutter, where he vomited violently.

Daphne was now crouched back against the wall of her room. Her eyes were going from Annie to Sarah. In spite of her drunken state, she realised what it was they wanted; there was no other reason why women such as these, would come to this place. She began to start making excuses.

"It wasn't my fault. How could I have stopped them? She hasn't been touched … I begged them not to hurt her … I would never have let them … Oh! No more!" Annie raised her hand again.

"Pamela is in room 47. Give me the key," she demanded.

"I haven't got it … I …' Annie reached for the second bottle of rum and poured the contents on the floor. The woman screamed in fury. Annie grabbed the woman by her mop of yellow hair and holding her securely, turned to the others. "John, you and Sarah go up to room 47; see if you can break the door in. Call out to Pamela; she'll recognize your voices and then won't be frightened"

There was a desperate struggle from Daphne, her arms swinging everywhere; Annie increased her hold on the hair.

"I'll keep this hell hound here," she continued, "if you can get into the room, carry Pamela down and take her to the car." Daphne, her hair held tightly in Annie grasp, reached for a cigarette from her desk and, without Annie being aware of what the woman was doing, lit the cigarette and inhaled deeply. In doing so, the thin gauzy stole she was wearing fell from her shoulders on to a chair and dangled onto the floor.

The cigarette glowed brightly and ash fell to the floor.

John and Sarah ran up the grimy and precarious staircase and soon the sound of crashing was heard and the terrified crying of a young girl. Annie then heard Sarah crying out as she called Pamela's name over and over, so Annie knew that they had found the child.

She would probably have left it at that, had she not seen the sneering contempt that was now on Daphne's face. She twisted her hand tighter in the mass of hair. Daphne shrieked:

"You'll never get away with this; I'll tell him all about it – and about you. That girl is nothing – she would have started earning money tonight, now it's all wasted. A bloody bastard who nobody wants! Why make a fuss over her? She'll get over it quickly enough."

Daphne paused to draw deeply on her cigarette, "I had promised a couple of chaps first go at her; they've already paid. But … Stop! What are you doing?"

Annie saw a whistle lying near the door. She realised what it could be used for, so still holding Daphne by the hair, she dragged her out the door of the office, blew the whistle as hard as she could, shouting at the top of her lungs. "*Police Raid*, everybody out quickly! You've got two minutes to get out! Run or you'll be locked up!"

There was pandemonium in the house. It seemed doors were opening and banging everywhere; girls began screaming and running down the stairs and into the street, with half their clothes done up and men, mainly seamen, trying desperately to get their pants back on. Annie saw with satisfaction that Sarah and John were lifting an almost unconscious girl into the car, so turned back to Daphne.

Annie, still holding tightly onto the mass of yellow hair, looked at the woman and her face registered her disgust. She transferred her hold from the hair to the front of Daphne's blouse. "You … revolt me!" she hissed into the woman's face and thrust her away with a great shove, as she turned to leave this terrible house.

Annie did not notice, immediately, that Daphne's cigarette had fallen with the violent push she had given the woman. The volatile liquor all over the floor burst instantly into flames, devouring in an instant the gauzy stole then leaping to the bed which was soon a ball of fire.

Daphne screamed in terror, realising her danger, grabbed her purse and ran shrieking from the building. The heat was horrendous.

Annie appalled, stared at what she had done; the inferno she had inadvertently created!

Trust me, she thought ruefully, to make a mess of it! She began to cough badly as she made her way outside in a hurry

As Annie got back into the car, John asked anxiously: "Mrs Watson, is that smoke coming from that dreadful place?"

"Why, I believe it is," Annie replied, coughing. "It's terrible how careless people are with matches, isn't it?"

She smiled at Pamela and gave her a big hug. "Well, let's get Pamela home and into bed; that's where she needs to be after a good bath. Peggy will see to that and Sarah you could stay with Pamela.

"I'm going to ask one more favour of you, John. I'm going to beg another ride in your car to the Falcon's house in Darlinghurst. If all goes well, I'll get a taxi and go back to your place, or else I'll go back to the Convent. I promised I'd be back by Vespers, that's at half past four o'clock. If I hurry, I'll make it."

John asked quietly: "Mrs Watson will you be long at the Falconi house. I could wait for you and then drive you to the station." Annie accepted, with gratitude, this generous offer. How kind people were when there was real trouble, she thought.

"I should be no more than fifteen minutes at the utmost, John. And, yes, I'd be very grateful for the offer; it's been quite a day."

John nodded his understanding.

Sarah spoke quietly to Annie: "If Pamela is safely back in bed, Annie, could I come with you to see Mother Benedicta – she's expecting me and I'm afraid of facing her alone. I'm not a Catholic, you see."

Annie actually laughed. "I'm sorry Sarah, I'd forgotten that you had to see Mother. Yes, of course you can come with me but first you'll have to come with me to the Falcon's house." She smiled at the nervous woman.

"But, Sarah, you have no need to be afraid of meeting Mother Benedicta. Just wait until you meet her; your fears will simply melt beneath the power of her love. She is unique – she just loves everybody."

Sarah appeared unconvinced, but was relieved that she would not be alone at the interview with the Mother Superior.

As they drove away, the building was well alight and people were running towards the fire. Very soon a fire engine passed them; they ignored it completely; but John raised his eyebrows, eyeing his extraordinary passengers in the rear vision mirror, with an amused smile.

55

The phones had rung almost continually in the Falcon's apartment. It seemed as if every call was yet another budget of bad news. First the news of the search underway for that wretched girl; then the shattering report of the desertion of the girls from Sarah's place and then Sarah's own disappearance – *with all the money*.

And so it had continued, place after place; he realised he was witnessing his life's work being destroyed. The final call had been the total destruction of Daphne's place by fire, *after* the rescue of that filthy brat from the Orphanage.

It was clear that Sarah was involved in all of this but there was another woman as well, who seemed to be far more powerful than Sarah. They had also involved the Parkers; that was dangerous; the son was a barrister and in with all the top cops.

The Falcon had also received a visit from Inspector Henderson – one who was, it seemed, totally impervious to bribes. That had been difficult and threatening. They couldn't do anything to him *yet*, he reasoned; they had no evidence to connect him to the abduction – unless Sarah talked.

Would she, he wondered? She had almost as much to lose as he had. He knew he could get away with the brothels – he had enough important men on his payroll to safeguard him there, but the abduction was another matter.

And, there was the money he had lost! Not just all the profit from the brothels, but also from his own safe! Who had been responsible for that? This was the greatest mystery of all; it was totally incomprehensible! He thought bitterly, you couldn't really trust anyone.

The Falcon had nearly suffered a heart attack when he had opened the safe Sunday morning, to take out a folder he needed. He had stared, astonished as he had been confronted with a yawning emptiness. All the money from the robbery was gone, together with a fair amount of extra cash – as well as other things, which were even more alarming.

The Falcon had immediately suspected his bodyguards, but when they were roused from sleep – after their early rising, they had happily returned to bed – their bewilderment was so obvious, that they had to be innocent. They were too dumb to be such actors as that!

Then his suspicion had turned to the only other obvious suspect: his grandson. He had sent for Lucky and asked him, coldly, to tell him the number of the safe. Lucky had stared at him in astonishment.

"Nonno," he had said at last, "you've never ever given me the combination; I don't know it. You promised, that if I pull off this big job this afternoon, then I would be a full partner, then you would tell me about a lot of things, including the safe."

The Falcon had stared searchingly at his grandson. It was certainly true what Lucky had said, and how else could he have gained any knowledge of the combination. The Falcon had never even written it down, but had trusted it to his memory as the only guarantee of safety. It was a mystery and the Falcon facing what looked like ruin, was in no mood for mysteries.

He sat perfectly still at his desk for a full hour. Tarzan and Jane were dismissed and the Falcon contemplated his future. He decided on a final plan. If this didn't work he would relocate to Melbourne. Sydney had become too dangerous to continue.

He would go to that unlucky convent this afternoon, disguised, and watch Lucky at work. If the boy did it well, then he would take the young chap – and his two guards; they were too stupid to be disloyal – and he'd then salvage what he could – and disappear.

There didn't seem anything else to do. The thought of Angelina crossed his mind, but he dismissed her quickly. She was only a mindless robot, with her rosary beads and her moronic piety – she was useless for everything, except working as a skivvy; he could easily get other skivvies, who would be just as good – even better.

Having decided on a plan of action, the Falcon rose from his desk and went to his bedroom. Carefully locking the door, he began his disguise transformation, firstly with the grey-white wig with straggling hair, which would hang over his collar. Then came the changes made to the face, the reshaping of the nose, the expert make-up which hollowed his cheeks; finally the old shabby clothes.

Later, he would leave the house by the side door, using a walking stick, and shuffle to the tram stop. He felt in his pocket for his vital necessities, a revolver and a large rosary. He smiled; the very picture of the devout and simple-minded old sinner. The thought amused him and – in spite of everything – he began to laugh.

It was good to be in action again; being on the edge of what could turn out to be a final disaster was stimulating. He wanted to release energy by running, but, remembering his role in time, he shuffled out of the house.

56

John Parker drove Annie and Sarah to the Falcon's house. Annie, who was aware how much he had already done for them, promised that they would be as quick as they could.

Once again, Annie, before she left the car, urged John when he did return home, to help Peggy keep Maureen at the house until she could arrange for help to arrive. She thought it useful to suggest that they get the local doctor to come and sedate the poor young woman; just to keep her there until Dr Gascoigne-Ridley could be contacted.

Annie led Sarah towards the steps of the house, noting its gigantic size. She also noticed – but Sarah did not – a face at the front window, watching an old man shuffling around from the corner of the house.

Annie nodded to him in passing, her brow furrowed; what was Angelina's connection with that elderly man? Perhaps, just an elderly neighbour? She shook her head; she was becoming too suspicious; seeing evil where there was none.

By the time she had rung the bell and waited for the door to be opened, she noted, absently, the old man had caught a tram and was lost to sight.

As the door slowly opened, the face of a frightened woman appeared for a moment in the opening. Angelina suddenly recognized Annie – this was the woman she had seen in the convent

Chapel that very morning. She tried quickly to slam the door shut. Annie, noting the move, shoved her shoulder in the opening.

"I think it would be advisable, Mrs Falconi for you to let us in. Otherwise, I shall have to go to the police and tell them that you were involved in the robbery. It was you who brought back the money to the nuns this morning at The Junction."

The elderly woman visibly crumpled at these words and, seizing her chance, Annie pushed open the door, taking the woman's arm, closed the door and led her inside and sat her down at her own table. Sarah tried to remain as unnoticeable, as possible.

When Angelina was seated, she lifted up her face and looked beseechingly at Annie. Annie was startled at the similarity – now, that she could see it clearly. What she had suspected, was now confirmed.

"Sister Mary Josepha's is your daughter isn't she?" she asked quietly. The woman began to cry. Annie reached over and took her hand.

"I know most of the story, Mrs Falconi and so does Mother Benedicta. You've nothing to fear from us. We know that Sister Josepha was forced to do what she did about the money, but you moved to save her, didn't you? You managed to get the money back somehow."

"I stole it from the safe, upstairs," the woman answered in a whisper. "If he ever finds out, he'll kill me, as he did my husband. *He killed his own son.*"

"Good God! He must be a monster! Then you are in great danger. We'll have to get you out of here. Is he home now?"

"No, I saw him go out just before you came in," she answered. "I hid her, you see, I didn't know what else to do."

"You mean, Sister Josepha?" the woman nodded. "I see, tell me about it. You did it cleverly; Sister has been safe for over fifteen years."

"Nearly eighteen years," corrected Angelina, "He," she moved her hand to point upwards, "destroyed the father and grandson is image of himself; he happy to follow in footsteps, but my poor Anna …"

"Anna?"

"Yes, is Sister Josepha's real name, Anna Falconi. He," again that gesture upstairs, "was determined that she be Madam of high class brothel he preparing, when she finish her nursing; my poor girl she beg me let her be nun. She always want to be nun, since she little girl."

Angelina blew her nose gently. "I was going to try save her from him, or die in attempt. A priest, then Bishop, made possible Anna Falconi disappear; Sister Mary Josepha be born. Her only sorrow was that she must leave young brother, Francis, behind. She love him. She made me promise send photos of him, as he growed up." The woman shuddered.

"I kept promise, send photos I could get of Francis, but I had to tell my dear girl of what he had become. I also remind her that the Falcon say he kill her, if ever find out where was."

"Have you had no contact with your daughter all these long years?" Annie could hardly believe what she was hearing; she wasn't sure the distraught woman knew what she was saying.

"Oh yes," Angelina nodded. "I write to her, send photos, as I say, but I not dare to visit in case he find out. He many men, including police, who works for him – I thought he follow me if I go. I write to her; she writes to me at Post Office, in another suburb. That is what we done all these years."

"So you always knew where she was?"

"Yes, but this morning, first time I be to Convent at The Junction. At Mass, I see my baby; I be so proud I want to die with thanks to God; He let me keep her safe for so long time."

"Mrs Jeffrey told me your name; it is Angelina, isn't it?" Annie asked abruptly. The woman looked surprised.

"Yes, Angelina Mary Falconi."

"Then you must call me Annie. I'm Annie Watson and this is

my friend, Sarah. The nun in charge of the Orphanage is my aunt. I'm here today, not only about the robbery, but about another young child …"

"Yes, Pamela Scott."

"How on earth did you know that?" Annie exclaimed, now really alarmed. She began to wonder if this day of shocks would ever end. To answer her question, Angelina stood up and beckoned the women to another room, and showed them the dumbwaiter.

"Every word they say I hear, if door open, this side," she explained. "That's how I learn about robbery. I no believe my ears when I hear that it was money for my daughter's Orphanage. I determined try to get money back."

Angelina then went on to explain to Annie how she had opened the safe.

"And," continued the older woman, "that's how I hear talk about poor little girl, Pamela, being took as well." Angelina hurried Annie into another room, filled with religious pictures. "Look, Annie," she gestured towards a little bunch of wilted flowers in a small vase, placed before a picture of the Virgin. "The little girl bring me … when that bad son of mine bring her here to meet me – a bunch of lavender! No one in my life ever give me flowers before."

Annie noticed that the poor woman's English continue to disintegrate as her emotions overflowed.

Angelina burst out crying again. "And then …two devils take her and hide her somewhere." Annie opened her mouth to interrupt the weeping woman – to tell her that Pamela was now safe – but was left gasping with shock, as Angelina's continued.

"And if not enough, to know … my son …he be ordered … kill nun at Convent today Vespers time …"

"WHAT!" Both Sarah and Annie shouted in horror. "Dear God, are you serious?" Annie continued. "Angelina, quickly, look at me! Tell me what you are talking about – do you really mean that a nun is to be murdered this afternoon?"

"Yes. That I tell you. I hear it be planned – through dumbwaiter."

"But, why? Who is to do the killing?"

"Well, Falcon – that's what he called – him, upstairs. He say Lucky, my son, to prove … enough strong – to take business over. He must do killing – this time … nun."

"And he definitely said it was to be at St Mary's did he?"

"Yes, definite. That's where I go, when you come. "

"You are certain that it is this afternoon?"

"Yes, Vespers … I heard them say."

Annie wrung her hands. "Angelina, do you happen to know if your son has left yet?"

"Yes, he go; him leave in grey van some time ago."

"Merciful God," Annie stammered clutching her wild hair, turned to Sarah "What on earth can we do?"

Sarah asked Angelina quickly, "Do you have a phone?" When Angelina nodded towards the corner of the room, Annie rushed to the instrument.

Annie tried the convent, only to get the engaged signal. She tried again and again but the phone was never free. I bet it's the Bishop on the phone with Aunt Benedicta about that damned secret file on Josepha, Annie reasoned.

She drummed her fingers in exasperation. As if the damn file mattered now! In desperation, Annie phoned her old friend, Inspector Peters, at Tavistock. He wasn't at the station, but as they knew her name well there, they gave her his home number.

When Annie rang there, it was to be told that the inspector had gone out for a walk. Annie, trying her hardest to speak calmly, left a message with the landlady to ask her to tell the inspector to ring the convent as quickly as he could, as a murder was about to be committed.

She also insisted that the woman write down her name; otherwise the inspector would think it was a hoax call.

Trying the convent once more, and finding the number still

engaged, Annie realised she had no more time to spare.

The car was still waiting outside the house so she bundled Angelina into her shawl, made sure the Italian woman had her large, black purse with her and ran out to the car. She then explained, at tremendous speed, the desperate situation to John, begging his assistance.

This, John granted immediately. Annie then put Sarah and Angelina into the back seat, asking Sarah to look after the agitated woman, then got in beside the driver, urging John to drive as if demented – if he wanted to save a bloodbath.

As the car sped away, Annie thanked him again, then took out her rosary and began to pray out aloud, oblivious of the others in the car. Soon, another voice joined hers – it was Angelina's.

57

Judge Maurice Bernstein turned to his wife, Janice. They were sitting in their conservatory which was pleasantly cool on this late summer day. They had finished an early afternoon tea and his mother-in-law, Eileen, had just left them.

"Janice, I'm worried about your mother," the judge spoke softly. "She's putting on her usual brave face, but I think she's still suffering from shock after that dreadful attack. I don't think it's wise to let her go to the Convent this afternoon, do you?"

"No, Maurie, I don't," answered Janice, grumpily, "but you try to stop her once she's made her mind up! She's a stubborn old biddy, and …" her voice broke, "she looks dreadful, Maurie; so dreadful, with her face all bruised and covered with plaster." The judge hastened to comfort his wife.

"I suppose you're right, dear, she's made up her mind to go, and that's that. Perhaps, it might be a good thing. You know, it all might help Eileen … calm her down, relax her."

"You're so good to her, Maurie," Janice reached down, and kissed her husband on the head. "I am very grateful. You're most probably right as well. Once she's home again she'll be so tired she'll be glad to be back in bed, then, please God, she might recover properly."

The Judge laughed softly. "And, while we're in the Chapel today, Janice, will you kindly pray to God that he might work a miracle, and stop Eileen's 'White Feather' campaign, once and for all."

"I'll do that, Maurie, but," she added, pulling a comical face, "it would require a pretty big miracle for that to happen. However, I'll do my best." She joined her husband's gentle laughter, thinking how lucky she was to have such a husband as Maurie. He cares for Eileen as though she were his own mother, she marvelled to herself. Very few other husbands do that – that was a little miracle in itself!

58

Inspector Peters, returning from his walk, was intercepted by his landlady, Mrs Carter.

"Excuse me, Inspector," she called from the kitchen, as she heard his steps in the hall. "There's been a strange call for you."

Bob Peters grimaced. He wondered if one day, perhaps when the war was over, he might be permitted to have just *one* day without being called out, when he was supposed to be off duty. Wearily he went into the kitchen. Mrs Carter was looking frightened. The inspector was immediately aware this was something different from the usual summons back to the station.

"Mrs Carter, what is it? What was the message?" The elderly woman looked at her favourite lodger with apprehension.

"I'm not sure if it was one of those ... hoax calls, I think you called them? Yes, that's right, a hoax call ..."

"What did it say? Was it a man or a woman?" Bob knew that most of the hoax calls came from hysterical women.

"It was a woman, she said that a murder is about to be committed at a convent."

"*WHAT*? She must be joking, or a lunatic. Did the caller leave a name?"

"Yes, she made me write it down carefully. It was," the elderly woman paused. "Now where did I put my glasses? I had them a minute or two ago. Oh yes, here they are." She picked up the note again. "It was a Mrs Annie Watson."

"Oh, my God!" shouted Peters. "Then it's for real. Quick Mrs Carter, did Mrs Watson say where the murder was to take place?"

The Inspector's reaction to the message shook his landlady. She never dreamed that it could be actually true. She was flustered and felt slightly dizzy. Sitting down quickly, she tried to remember everything that frightened woman had said on the phone. All she could remember was the name of the place.

"I'm sorry, Inspector, it's all a bit of a muddle in my head, but I think the place was the big Orphanage at The Junction."

"Right! I'm sorry to have startled you Mrs Carter. Please let me use the phone now; every minute could be precious." Bob Peters rushed to the phone and had begun to dial the station when he thought of another thing. He called to his landlady. "Mrs Carter, did Mrs Watson mentioned a time by any chance?"

"Good God! Yes, she did. I clean forgot. She said at Vespers – I think that was the name – which I think she said was at half past four o'clock."

Peters looked up at the clock on the hall wall and swore mildly. He contacted the station and spoke briefly to his second in command, Sergeant Pierce. As quickly as he could, he managed to put Pierce in the picture, but added, "Pierce, we'll never get there in time; it's after four o'clock now.

"Ring the police at the Junction for back-up and send a car for me at once – with the fastest driver we have. I'll try to contact the convent while I'm waiting."

59

Lucky Falconi quietly entered the Chapel street door and found two elderly people already there. He chose the back pew, with the seat he had used before; closest to the aisle and the door. Behind him, near the entrance door, was the large statue of St Joseph, which would partially conceal him.

From his position, he had a perfect view of the whole Chapel. He knelt down, slightly raising his shoulders, which helped disguise his shape, then removing his thin, grey-silk scarf, wrapped it loosely around his hands which rested on the back of the pew in front of him. It looked as if he were simply holding his scarf in his hands – there certainly was a little breeze blowing in through the open door, but it was still a very warm afternoon; you certainly didn't need to wear a scarf.

He let his rosary beads hang from the scarfed hands, finishing the picture of a devout, and serious, young man.

In fact, Lucky found the scarf an excellent cover for hiding the gun safely in his hands; if he could keep the gun there, until it was ready to fire, it would be a breeze. He would most probably need to stand up as he fired; it depended whether there were any other people in front of him; it wouldn't matter, if it were seen – he'd be gone in a flash after he had fired.

But, for the moment, it was resting securely on the wooden rail of the next pew.

60

The Judge, Janice and Eileen, glad to be out of the sun, hurried in through the open door of the Chapel, surprised at how cool it was compared, to the outside temperature. The Judge led Eileen to the front pew.

Lucky felt a severe jolt in his stomach, when he recognized the woman he had attacked. He also knew the Judge by sight – the Falcon had insisted that Lucky do so, when the judge had visited him. What the hell were they doing here, he thought angrily? The bloody old hanging judge! Him coming to Church! That was a joke.

But why is that woman with him? What's the connection between them?

Lucky was painfully aware, that if the woman turned around, she could see him – that could be dangerous. Lucky bent his head even lower, moved his body back closer, into the shadow of the large statue, while his lips muttered, as if he were deep in his prayers.

Five more people hurried into the Public Chapel while somewhere a nun was ringing a sweet-sounding bell. Not long to go now, Lucky thought. More people arrived taking up most of the empty places. Lucky had to stand up to let a couple of people get into his pew, holding the gun carefully, in the scarf, against his body, and smiling politely as he did so.

He began to worry; he had never expected to find so many people – he knew he would have to stand up to fire now. Keep on your toes, he gave orders to himself. He looked up, as yet another old man, shuffled into the pew opposite him at the back. That's funny, he thought, he looks slightly familiar; perhaps he was the old chap who was in here the other day when he was here.

Lucky shook his head slightly; he was becoming distracted: dismiss the bloke from your mind, he's not important; concentrate on the job – *nothing* else matters, and *nobody* else either; just do what you have been told to do.

The bell continued its insistent ringing… ringing… ringing.

61

"My dear child," Mother Benedicta said, helping Sister Mary Luke out of bed and adjusting her clothing, "are you sure this is what you want to do? Sister Josepha is with me; she will bring you down to the Chapel if that's what you really want, but I don't think it's wise, do you?"

The frail, white, trembling form of the young nun, her face drawn with pain, raised herself upright. "Please, Mother," she whispered. "Just for this one time – to be with the Sisters."

"Oh course, if that's what you want my child; make sure you wear your slippers, don't bother with shoes." Mother Benedicta released her hold on Sister Luke and let Sister Josepha take her place and complete Luke's dressing by adjusting the cream-coloured mantle the Sisters wore for Sundays and special days. The long, beautiful cloak fell gently to the ground as Luke stood up, holding on tightly to Josepha. Mother Benedicta still hesitated; desperately worried for the dying Luke. She forced herself to speak cheerfully.

"Sisters, you know I must be down there before the bell stops ringing, so I've got to run." She attempted to make a little convent joke: "But you needn't be telling anyone about me running now, will you?"

They smiled; Benedicta began to leave, then turned back briefly. "Sister Josepha, if there's any need to return, come back at once, or ask for help from the Sisters, especially Sister Raphael – she's the doctor – if you need it. Leave the Chapel at any time during Vespers – you have my total permission, so just use your common sense. Is that understood?"

The two nuns nodded: Mother Benedicta lifted up her voluminous skirts, and ran until she was in sight of the other Sisters. She then moderated her walk into a rapid, but seemly, pace.

Sister Mary Margaret came up to her, babbling something incomprehensible about a frightening phone call. Benedicta questioned the nun sharply, but Sister Margaret confessed she couldn't understand what it meant at all – she thought it was just a nuisance call, but the caller had said he was an Inspector Peters.

Mother Benedicta stood stock still. If Bob Peters had called her, it would definitely have been something serious. Why hadn't God given this silly, idiotic, woman some brains, she muttered to herself in irritation?

Well, it was too late now. The bell had stopped ringing and she was not yet in the Chapel; she'd deal with it after Vespers.

Mother Benedicta walked sturdily into the Chapel, genuflected to the altar and stumped down the long aisle between the choir-stalls to her special stall, near the grill.

She noticed, with a quick glance, that the public Chapel seemed crowded today. That was fairly unusual – for Vespers especially. After she had climbed the two steps into her stall, she stood while the rest of the Sisters came into the Chapel.

They genuflected to the altar, bowed to their Superior and then took their own places in the choir stalls.

There was the sound of rustling as the nuns stood waiting for the Superior to begin. Benedicta began to sing in her strong, old voice: "Deus, in adiutorium meum intende" O God, come to my assistance; the Sisters replied: "Domine, ad adiuvandum me festina" Oh Lord, make haste to help me.

The doxology was intoned, and finally, the cantors for the week began to sing the Antiphon for the first psalm:

"Dixit Dominus Domino meo: Sede a dextris meis" The Lord said to my Lord, sit on my right.

The chanting faltered slightly as there was the sound – from the street outside the public Chapel – of people running. At the same instant, two Sisters appeared at the Chapel door near the altar; Sister Josepha was leading, half carrying, Sister Luke. The nuns continued the psalm they were singing, but every nun had one eye on her book and one watching Josepha, as she lifted Luke, after the poor woman had tried to genuflect. The two nuns both turned slowly to face the Superior and bowed.

Lifting up her head Josepha, looking straight down the centre of the Chapel into the public area; stood transfixed:

She was staring at … **HER BROTHER** – she recognized him instantly!

With sudden, terrifying clarity and comprehension she understood her terrifying dreams – why he now stood with a gun in his hand!

He was going to kill her … *she was about to die*!

Josepha screamed piercingly in her terror. While frantically keeping her eyes on her brother, she dragged Sister Luke desperately out of the range of fire, behind her back and shouted:

"NO Francis, NO! … DON'T! … please, Francis … you are my BROTHER!"

Sister Mary Luke's keen eyes had seen what Josepha had seen and with an astonishing gathering of her last strength, she resisted Josepha's efforts to shield her and – for a moment only – stood exposed, her arms outstretched, shielding Josepha, as the gun exploded.

Josepha shrieked again, this time in gasping horror, as Sister Luke slid from her arms with the front of her guimp turning red with blood as it burbled out from her chest; her mantle rapidly changing colour.

Following almost immediately, another shot rang out, deafening in the enclosed space, reverberating round and round the Chapel, leaving the people deaf, dazed and throwing them into screaming panic.

The second bullet slammed into Sister Josepha's chest; her body arched upwards and backwards her face held in a rictus of agony … then … ever so slowly, she began to crumple and die.

She fell slowly at the feet of the fatally wounded Sister Luke, her body jerked in a convulsive movement, and then lay still.

Sister Mary Josepha was dead.

Sheer terror-induced pandemonium ensued.

62

As Annie, Angelina, Sarah and John were running from the car towards the street door of the Chapel, they almost collided with Inspector Peters and Sergeant Pierce coming from the opposite direction; the Junction police following them. All eight people crammed into the door at the same time.

They were just in time to hear Sister Josepha's words, and then the gun shots nearly deafened them, leaving them confused and disoriented.

With their ears still ringing, Annie and Peters shoved forward through the near hysterical crowd of people, but Angelina had burrowed her way through to the grill before any of them. She stood clutching the bars with her hands, her face twisted in anguish, uttering loud shrieks of despair.

Most of the people in the public section were half-seated, half-standing; all in a state of shock, many screaming loudly in hysteria.

Suddenly, Annie saw a tall elderly woman, with plaster on her face in the front pew, suddenly stand up.

Eileen deliberately turned to look back, towards the door. Her eyes sought the gunman and quite clearly she saw *who* it was. The woman's eyes opened wide in horror as she recognized him. Pointing her whole arm in the direction, she shouted loudly over the dreadful noise:

"Judge, that's the man who attacked me ... Oh, somebody get

him! He's the murderer! He's …"

Whatever else poor Eileen was going to say, was cut short by a gasp of pain as Lucky shot her. The woman fell back, bleeding profusely from her face. The people near Lucky, now realising that they were near a maniac, crushed themselves into the corners of the pews, and under them, trying to escape from him.

Lucky, aware now that he had the police to contend with, knew his only hope of escape was to shoot it out. He raised his weapon again, warning everyone to stay well clear, or they would die.

He edged his way to the door with the statue at his back; the police, Sarah and John who were now in front of him, were helpless while he had the gun aimed at them.

However, for one moment, he was exposed on his own and that was enough for Angelina. She held in her hand the gun she had found and filched from the Falcon's safe and shouted to her son to stay perfectly still, or she would shoot him.

Lucky turned an astonished face to his mother, his mouth gaping open; nothing had prepared him for this.

Angelina had both hands on the gun; it was wavering dangerously, but it was definitely pointing at her son.

Following on his shock, Lucky was filled with savage fury. "Why, you slobbering moron," he shouted, "you think you can stop me!" He raised his weapon and his finger tightened on the trigger. Angelina seeing what was to happen, closed her eyes and fired.

There were then double explosions of sounds, firstly of the guns and then of gigantic thuds as though the ceiling had fallen in. This left everyone disoriented, ears ringing, the screams becoming louder – while two elderly women fainted and fell between the pews.

At the shot from Angelina's gun, Lucky crashed to the floor, and lay still.

But, Angelina had missed Lucky entirely; she had shattered the huge statue of St Joseph behind him. The heavy statue, in falling, had struck Lucky, knocking him unconscious to the floor and causing his gun to fire, in his convulsive shock. The bullet had gone through the grill, narrowly missed Mother Benedicta and leaving a round jagged hole in her wooden stall.

As soon as Lucky fell, the police pounced on him. They quickly put manacles in place and removed the gun, but it seemed that he would be unconscious for quite a while.

Angelina standing at the grill, still holding the gun with both hands, spoke in a quavering voice. "Mr Policemen, don't let old man in grey wig escape. Don't let him make you fool: he be the Falcon. He ordered murder of Sisters by my son ... he planned both robbery and kidnap poor child, little Pamela. He be armed ... be careful."

She spoke then to the old man struggling now to get out of the Chapel. "Falconi, if you try get away, I kill you. You kill my husband; you kill my daughter. You evil ...now my son gone too... now, you ... nothing ... left." She attempted to laugh, which quickly turned to sobbing. "All for nothing ... all evil you done ... for nothing, nothing, at all ... no one left ... now ... no one ... I have ... no one now ... I ..." Angelina, her eyes glazing, raised the pistol to her head.

Annie who was closest to her, shouted, "No, Angelina, no!" and grabbed her. They struggled, and with all her strength, Annie pulled the gun-hand away from the distraught woman. The gun exploded, but the bullet went harmlessly into the ceiling, causing plaster to cascade down on the distraught people underneath.

Throwing the gun down, Angelina turned to Annie and buried her face in her breast; her anguished sobbing reverberating in the confined space, mingling with the terror of the frenzied screaming.

As the police and John managed to overcome the Falcon, Angelina let go of Annie, and slid to the floor still holding the bars of the grill, crying for her murdered child, her baby.

63

The screaming and shouting from the public Chapel and the sounds of great struggling, followed by more explosions of gunfire, filled the Sisters in their stalls with terror. They were frightened and bewildered, not knowing what had happened.

All they were really aware of was that they were looking, with unbelieving eyes, incredulously, at two of their own Sisters lying on the floor in front of them, unbelievably *murdered*. With this realisation, many began to scream in shock, while others began to cry loudly, some near the point of hysteria.

A senior girl from the girls' section of the chapel had pushed forward and had seen the carnage in the chapel. She then told the girls what had happened; their precious Sister Luke, had been murdered! They began to cry loudly; soon they had joined the Sisters in their screaming.

Mother Benedicta, after the first moments of utter paralysing shock, leapt from her stall and oblivious to any danger, actually ran to the dying nuns. Mother Benedicta showed then why she had remained Superior for so many years. She quickly saw that Josepha was dead, but Luke was still conscious.

As she knelt on the floor she pulled Josepha to her side and the dying Luke into her arms. Kneeling there with her two children, Benedicta issued a series of commands in her old, loud, strong voice which trembled with emotion, but brooked no delay.

"Sister Michael, get the priest, then the doctor; ring the police and the Bishop – in that order – as fast as you can.

"The Sisters who are nurses, come here at once! One stay here with Sister Luke, the others go to the public Chapel; there could be people wounded there, perhaps you can help. Sister Raphael, send a Sister for your medical bag and go to the public chapel.

"Sister Agatha, open the grill and remain at the door.

"Sister Therese and Sister Clare, do not attempt to finish Vespers; begin the Litany for the Dying for Sister Mary Luke *immediately*; she is still alive. After the Litany, begin the Office of the Dead for the two Sisters.

"Sister Mary Peter, ring the Passing Bell; it must toll twice, twenty four times for Sister Luke, thirty-five times for Sister Josepha.

"Sister Genevieve, go to the girls' Chapel and stop them screaming. Explain to them what has happened; tell them to begin the Rosary for the dead immediately." Benedicta's voice rose and she spoke sharply, as she addressed her community:

"Sisters, I *order* you to stop that unseemly screaming immediately. You will answer the Prayers for the Dying in a proper manner, then we shall begin the Office of the Dead."

The two cantors quickly found the places in their books, then, with shaky voices, began to chant the Litany as ordered:

Kyrie eleison. Christe eleison. Kyrie eleison.

While Mother Benedicta held the dying Luke in her arms, Sister Ursula, a nurse, laid the dead Sister Josepha down reverently. She used her own white handkerchief to tie up the chin to the top of Josepha's head, thus changing the face of terror into peaceful tranquillity. Ursula folded the dead nun's hands across her chest, arranged the cream mantle across the bloodied guimp and took the crucifix from Sister's waist, placing it into the lifeless fingers. She straightened the legs so that Sister Josepha was now lying decently, with her clothes carefully adjusted.

Sancta Maria ... ... ora pro ea

Sister Mary Luke was still alive, but only just. Benedicta didn't try to hide the tears that fell as she held the young woman in her arms. Sister Luke looked up at her and smiled, her huge eyes beseeching the Superior to understand something. Benedicta bent down as far as her starched collar would allow. "Yes, my child. God will come for you with joy; the angels are waiting for you, I am sure of that, my dearest child. Is there anything …?"

Sister Luke smiled again, and mouthed the words which the Superior immediately understood. "Yes, our darling child; it is the Magnalia Dei, the glorious work of God – *you* are the precious Work of God." Sister Luke's chest rose sharply; she sighed gently … slowly and, as her eyes became fixed, she exhaled very slowly, and her head fell to one side.

She was dead … Mother Benedicta wept openly crushing the dead body of Luke – her youngest child – to her breast.

Omnes sancti Angeli et Archangeli … … … orate pro ea

Mother Benedicta stayed with her two dead daughters on the floor of the Chapel until the end of the Litany, her face tragic. She was utterly indifferent to the blood of the dying Luke spreading across the large white starched guimp she wore, as she joined in the responses.

The huge Passing Bell began its solemn tolling, the deep, reverberating toll counting out the years of each nun's life. The sound swirled round and round, echoing through the Chapel, up to the ceiling and booming above the surrounding streets, becoming part of the Litany itself.

Sancte Abel … … … ora pro ea   *Dong-ng-ng!*

As the Litany progressed Mother Benedicta found that Annie had come through the grill door and was kneeling with her on the floor. Annie had her arm around the old nun and was holding her tightly, while she, too, joined in the responses.

Omnes Sancti et Sanctae Dei … … … intercedite pro ea   *Dong-ng-ng!*

Annie did not come through alone. The elderly Italian woman had come through the same door, and was holding Sister Mary Josepha in her arms, her grief overwhelming. She said, softly, only two words, over and over and over: "My baby, my baby, my baby…"

Propitius esto … … … libera eam, Domine   *Dong-ng-ng!*

Inspector Bob Peters and Sergeant Pierce had come in with Angelina Falconi and as the priest had arrived, Peters gently took the body of Angelina's daughter from the arms of her mother, to enable the old priest, Father O'Shea, to anoint the body with trembling hands and speech. He was very old, and was himself in a state of shock. He then anointed Sister Luke.

The Litany wound its way through the Saints of the Church and finished as it had started:

Kyrie eleison. Christe eleison. Kyrie eleison.   *Dong-ng-ng!*

Annie and the Superior knelt together as the priest said the solemn commendation: 'Go forth, O Christian souls out of this world …'

When the last Blessing had been given, Sister Clare lifted up her glorious voice in the beautiful: 'In Paradisum.'

The huge bell continued to toll.   *Dong-ng-ng!*

The other Sisters quickly joined Sister Clare and when they had finished singing, Mother Benedicta gave instructions for the Office of the Dead to begin immediately then excused herself from Chapel.

The old nun struggled to her feet, grateful for the use of Annie's strong arm, and nodded to Peters, "I'll be with you in a minute, Inspector."

The cantors quickly turned to the correct places in their books and the sombre Office of the Dead began, while two Sisters who worked in the Sacristy, placed candles on the floor at the head and feet of their slain companions.

Requiem aeternam dona eis, Domine   *Dong-ng-ng!*

With the Office underway, Mother Benedicta could leave it no longer. She had to deal with the police and then discover what on earth had happened in the public Chapel. It was her convent; a House under her care – the whole situation was one in which she was solely and completely responsible: before God, the Church and the civil authorities.

Meanwhile, Inspector Peters and Sergeant Pierce had gently lifted Angelina to her feet and led her away to where policemen from The Junction police station were waiting to receive her.

Et lux perpetua luceat eis   *Dong-ng-ng!*

Mother Benedicta hurried to the public chapel where the police had the Falcon already handcuffed to the metal grill where he struggled violently and hopelessly. Benedicta faced the policeman: "Inspector, I'm ready now. Thank you for waiting."

Requiescant in pace ... Amen   *Dong-ng-ng!*

64

Inspector Peters and Sergeant Pierce, with the aid of police from The Junction, had taken the names of the people who had been in the public Chapel and let them go home. Those who had been injured had been examined briefly by the nursing Sisters and told to sit outside on the steps to recover after their terrible shock. Sister Raphael moved among them, her stethoscope hanging from her neck.

Shocked as the congregation were, they were only too happy to be able to leave. A number of them sat outside on the steps for only a short time, but as soon as they were beginning to recover they were anxious to get away – to go home – away from this horror. Apart from the Falcon and the police, it was only the Judge, Angelina, Sarah and John who were still there, when Mother Benedicta came through the door in the grill with Annie.

With the constant, slow, tolling of the Passing Bell, everyone adjusted their speech to the silence between the strokes.

The Superior was just in time to make the sign of the Cross over the body of the unconscious Lucky as he was carried out to a waiting ambulance. She looked at the young man with compassion.

"God have mercy on him, Inspector. Apparently, from what Annie has just whispered to me, he was merely carrying out the orders of this man." She surveyed the tall man still locked to the grill. "We will pray for you; also for your grandson."

The Falcon looked at her and spat with contempt.

Benedicta turned to Josepha's mother, Angelina. She came forward and took the sobbing woman in her arms. "Annie told me what happened, my dear. I never knew that poor Sister Josepha's mother was still alive."

Benedicta's voice became firmer. "I thank God you missed when you tried to shoot your son; St Joseph took over and saved you from that."

Benedicta looked at Peters. "What is the situation regarding Sister Josepha's mother – this poor woman? I understand she actually tried to shoot her own son, but she was defending herself in the end, wasn't she?" She paused and then pleaded. "Surely she has suffered enough."

Inspector Peters replied, gravely. "That is undoubtedly true, but she did bring the gun with her, which indicates premeditation. However, you could well argue that, knowing of the proposed murder of her daughter, she was simply trying to protect her child."

The Inspector looked squarely at the Mother Superior. "Mother, you know it is not up to me; it is for the courts to decide guilt, or otherwise."

The judge intervened. "My Lady Benedicta, you do not know me, but you know Eileen Hodges; she is my mother-in-law. She was one of those who were shot by the young man – fortunately, only a flesh wound. She's been taken away by ambulance. I am Judge Maurice Bernstein, and I want to assure you that I shall personally see that this poor woman has the best legal counsel available."

The Judge went on: "I know the whole story and I shall be proud to cover the total costs myself. Yes, she did threaten to shoot her son, but let me say that he was going to kill his mother as you said, there is no doubt about that, so it really could be seen as a case of self defence.

"The young man is an evil, a very evil man, but through the poor woman's desperate action, she has provided the proof which makes it possible for the police to actually charge that man at the grill for the very first time – he was the instigator of the whole wicked plan.

"He is one of the most dangerous men in Australia."

The Superior nodded her understanding and, keeping her arm around the weeping Angelina, spoke quietly.

"Thank you, your Honour. I can only thank you for your compassion. When Angelina has finished at the station, if she is free to do so, could you please bring her back here? She has no one else. She could stay here with us for a few days, and be welcome. She and I could watch by her daughter tonight."

Benedicta turned to the other strangers and raised her eyebrows to Annie.

Annie introduced John Parker, the barrister, who informed Benedicta of Pamela's rescue. He added that he would be happy to join with the Judge in trying to get Angelina completely acquitted.

"She has removed the two people who organized and directed the drugging and kidnapping of that totally innocent young girl. Mrs Falconi's statement, when she gets to the station, will finish the Falcon at last." The young man's lips were compressed in a determined line. "I will try my best to see that the Falcon never gets out of gaol in his lifetime."

Looking quickly at the Judge, who nodded, John added: "I think it is quite definite that Mrs Falconi will be allowed to return here, after she has given her statement."

Annie was wearily leaning against the grill, still suffering from shock, but after John had spoken, she began to introduce Sarah to her aunt, but Mother Benedicta forestalled her. "One look at Sarah was all I needed," she smiled, and kissed the frightened woman. "You must stay here at St Mary's until things are sorted out. I am so grateful to God that Pamela is safe. I believe that it is through your efforts that this has come about."

Sarah protested and said if it hadn't been for Annie, nothing would have been done.

The van arrived to take away the Falcon. He left between two police men cursing God, the nuns, and Mother Benedicta in particular. Inspector Peters and Sergeant Pierce, taking Angelina, in their car with them, left for the Station to lay the charges against the gangster.

Benedicta sat down suddenly. "I'm not as young as I was," she muttered. John Parker and the Judge also left for the station after taking their leave of the Superior, who immediately stood up and graciously thanked them. Finally, the women were left alone.

"Well, now they're all gone," Benedicta said, "come up to my office and we'll just sit for a minute or two. I think we all need it and you can fill me in on all the things I still need to know.

"Come in by the grill door; I'll lock the outside door as well as this one. We don't have much time before the wretched press start hounding us. They will have a field day with what happened here today."

The three women went into the Chapel; Annie and Sarah paused by the side of the two dead nuns and waited, respectfully, while Benedicta said her own silent good-bye to her daughters in Christ.

The Passing Bell sounded its final note: *Dong-ng-ng!*

65

In Mother Benedicta's office, Annie and Sarah waited quietly, while the Superior dealt with all the details that attended the deaths of the nuns. They were introduced to Sister Mary Michael who would have the lion's share of organizing the Funeral, notifying the relatives and arranging the watching by the Sisters until the Funeral was over.

"The sacristan Sisters are cleaning and dressing the bodies, now, Mother, with the help of two of the nurses." Sister Michael informed her Superior. "They will be presentable by the time Sister Luke's parents arrive and be lying on catafalques.

"I've arranged for the first four nuns to Watch beside the body for the next two hours. The others can then take it in turns. But I need your approval for a request from the senior girls. They have asked if they could share in the night Watching – especially for Sister Luke," the nun's voice trembled, but quickly recovered, "she was a favourite of theirs."

"Permission given, Sister," Benedicta responded, "but not excessive; we don't want sick nuns, or girls, on our hands, but let the girls know how grateful I am for their offer."

She checked on her fingers. "I think everything is covered. I'll speak to the Bishop – he'll be here this evening and I'm sure you have contacted the Undertakers?" Sister Michael nodded.

"Good. I'm afraid that you, Sister Michael, with Sister Clare and I, will have to share the burden of the press ourselves.

"Sister Agatha will do her best at the gate, but warn the girls to be on their guard not to say anything to any reporter, except that it was a great tragedy, and that they don't know the details."

She was interrupted by the arrived of two senior girls with a tray with tea things. "Ah, here's some relief. Wouldn't you know my children would know just what we needed?" The elderly nun smiled at the two red-eyed girls who, silently and shyly, set out the tea and then quietly left the room. Benedicta turned to Annie. "You pour out, dear. Sister Michael, would you care to stay? You may if you wish."

The second-in-charge shook her head expressing her thanks, and hurried from the room. She knew full well, as did the Superior, what the next few days would be like.

Mother Benedicta then took the cup of tea from Annie's hand and said: "Now, all the details, Annie as fast as you can. Sarah, you add your information as well; I don't have much time. I want to watch during the night myself, not for Sister Luke, but for poor Sister Josepha – I have failed her; she has been carrying a terrible burden for fifteen years and I was not even aware of it. We could have carried it together – I could have protected her, had I known.

"It is my own fault, not hers, God have mercy on that poor, poor, lonely nun."

Benedicta shook herself like a plump puppy. "Now, off you go, tell me everything I need to know Annie."

"Before I begin, Aunt," Annie began, "I must get the problem of Maureen Thomson fixed up. I've promised the mother. This is what it is all about ..." Annie recounted the rescue of Pamela Scott, due to the information given by the drug addict who risked her life in coming to them, with the news of Pamela's whereabouts.

"I promised the family, Aunt, that we would try to help the poor tragic girl. Would you let me use your name in asking Dr Gascoigne-Ridley for help?"

"Of course, Annie, tell Ernest I particularly want him to help the girl. You can take that for granted. Now tell me what happened after you left here to try to find Pamela."

Annie reported all the things that had happened in that extraordinary day, and praised Sarah for her heroic stand against the Falcon. The Superior turned to Sarah.

"My dear child, I don't know how you will get on with Pamela. It'll be a tremendous shock to her now, to know she has a mother – she might be resentful of the past, that's possible, but I think she'll be simply thrilled to death to know she has a mother. As I understand it, you no longer have a home, so as I suggested earlier, you stay with us for a while.

"We'll bring Pamela here for a few days to recover and you two can get a chance to know each other."

Sarah expressed her thanks, but added worriedly, "Mother, I have to earn my living, so I must start looking around for a job."

"I understand," Benedicta replied. "Well it so happens that with poor Sister Josepha gone, I need someone used to financial dealings. So, for at least a short while, you could earn your keep," she smiled gently, as she said this, "until you can find a proper job with good money – with some prospects – the prospects here are not very promising! In fact, they're non-existent. What do you think, Annie?"

"It sounds perfect," Annie replied, "at least, for the short term, anyhow." She stood up. "Aunt, I'm going to get off home. You have enough on your plate without having to worry about me. I'll phone Ernest before I leave here, also the Parkers – they'll be wondering where their son, John, is. Sarah can use my room here in the convent, if that's all right with you."

Mother Benedicta stood up and embraced her niece. "Annie, what would I have done without you? I'll never forget this. Give my love to the kids, and to poor long-suffering Sam." Her elderly exhausted face creased for a moment into a smile.

Annie smiled with her, then kissed Sarah and left the building – neatly avoiding four reporters who were waiting at the gate ready to pounce on anyone leaving the premises.

66

Annie arrived home in the early evening. The near-autumn wind was cool and she was grateful to see that Sam had the fire lit, even though it was not strictly necessary.

As she came through to the living room, her husband jumped up. "You're home, at last, love. We'd given up hope of ever seeing you again. Penny said you had run away with a wealthy Yank, while Billy was certain you had taken the veil!"

"And you, Sam?" Annie smiled at her husband.

"No, I said you'd be just lying around, being waited on hand and foot, driving the nuns crazy, being a damn nuisance to everyone, but having a wonderful lazy time." Sam held his wife at arm's length. "Now, tell the truth Annie, which one of us was right?"

"Oh, that's easy, Sam darling. You were, of course." She smiled as she pulled off her gloves. "A wonderful holiday – nothing happening, and nothing to do."

Sam looked at Annie searchingly. "I don't believe a word of it. With your track record, you most probably burnt the whole place down."

"Well, Sam, you're close dear, but it wasn't *the whole* place." Annie pulled off her hat, thrust her hated gloves in it, and threw the hat into a corner.

67

One week later, Annie knelt before the grill in the dark confessional at Tavistock Catholic Church. She was nervous, and glad of the darkness, as well as the fact that the curtain, inside the grill, meant she would not see the priest. She was hoping desperately that her voice would not be recognized.

It was a feeble hope; after all, Father Reilly was a relative, as well as a friend; he knew her well.

After the priest had finished with the person on the other side of the Confessional, the little door opened and the old voice spoke through the grill: "Yes, my child?"

"Bless me Father for I have sinned ..." Hearing the voice, the priest sighed windily. He recognized immediately who was there; he steeled himself mentally. This would be a peculiar confession, as all Annie's were – he would need his wits about him. His voice sharpened.

"*What* have you done, *now*?"

"Nothing much, Father. I've been ...um ... playing ... er ...with fire ..."

"And?"

"It wasn't exactly my fault. Now, I don't want to teach you your job, Father, but you know you have to have the *intention* of doing something gravely sinful for it to be a serious sin, but Spirits have always been a mystery to me ..."

"Spirits? You don't mean to tell me you are playing around with the *Occult* are you? This is very serious…"

"No, no… nothing like that. The *other* spirits…you know…"

"No, I don't know, that's why I'm asking you …"

"You know… Rum …"

"Rum? You've been drinking? That is outrageous. Now, listen to me…."

"No I haven't had a drop. You see, I didn't know about Bacardi Rum …"

"Bacardi Rum? What's Bacardi Rum got to do with it?"

"It's flammable …"

"Of *course* it's flammable! Oh dear, I think I'm beginning to have one of my turns. Well, go on…"

"I … um … I …well … I… burnt …something"

"Let's shorten this, shall we? Did you have a cooking accident? Burn something with Rum on the stove?"

"Not exactly. But I did burn … something…"

"Get to the point. What did you burn?"

"Well ….here goes! *I burnt down a house.*"

There was a loud thud from the other side of the closed grill.

"Father … Father … *Father Reilly! … Are you all right?*"

***